JU...

a...
TRAVELLER

Ashling Donnellan

owns

this

O.K.

JUDITH
and the
TRAVELLER

Mike Scott

Reprinted 1992
First published 1991 by
WOLFHOUND PRESS
68 Mountjoy Square
Dublin 1

Wolfhound Press receives financial assistance from The Arts Council/
An Chomhairle Ealaíon, Dublin, Ireland.

British Library Cataloguing in Publication Data
Scott, Mike
    Judith and the traveller
    I. Title
    823.914 [F]

    ISBN 0-86327-299-1

This book is fiction. All characters, incidents and names have no
connection with any persons living or dead. Any apparent
resemblence is purely coincidental.

Cover design: Joanne Finegan
Typesetting: Seton Music Graphics Ltd., Bantry, Co. Cork.
Printed by Cox & Wyman Ltd., Reading, Berkshire.

For Celia, Eilís and Liam,
fellow travellers . . .

Saturday 28th July

1

You were supposed to cry at weddings because you were happy—not because you felt as if your heart was breaking.

If one more person asked her if she was delighted or told her how lucky she was, or said how pleased they were, then she was going to scream. She was not delighted, she was not lucky, and she most definitely was not pleased!

She also had a pain in her face from smiling at people she didn't know, and for the countless photographs. This had to be the most photographed wedding in Dublin: as well as the two official wedding photographers, there was a third cameraman making a video, and there were three press photographers present, two from the Irish newspapers and one from an English tabloid. But, she supposed, when a wealthy British banker marries an equally wealthy Irish heiress, there was bound to be some interest.

It turned the whole day into a circus!

Judith Meredith twisted around in the limousine to look back at the crowds gathered at the church, some of them still waving, throwing confetti and rice, while others were making an undignified dash for their cars to be the first in line behind the white Rolls Royce carrying the bride and groom, and the three gleaming black Bentleys which carried the immediate family. The young woman leaned forward and stared at the long white car directly in front. She could see her father and her new step-mother through the back window. They were kissing.

Judith turned away in disgust.

It was wrong! Her mother was barely two years dead; her father shouldn't have married, not so soon . . . and certainly not to that woman!

Judith Meredith sank back into the soft leather seat, lace-gloved hands twisting her bridesmaid's posy of tiny red roses and heather to pieces. The lavender in the posies matched the colour of her dress. Her older brother and his wife were sitting across from her, chatting excitedly about the wedding. They didn't seem to think that there was anything wrong . . . so why should she?

Was it because her father was marrying their mother's best friend?

Or was it because she had had her father all to herself for the past two years? It had fallen to her to remind him when to pay the bills on time, when to renew the television licence, when the car needed a service. Maxwell Meredith might be the chairman of one of the largest independent banking organisations in the world; he might do million pound deals every day of the week, but he was completely useless when it came to the ordinary day-to-day running of a house.

When her mother had died two years ago, well, two years, two months and eight days ago—Judith continued to count the days—she had just turned thirteen. When all the fuss had died down, when all the sympathisers had gone away, when her elder brother had returned to his wife and family and her sister had returned to Canada, Judith had been the one left behind to look after her father. He had come to depend on her.

Everything had been fine until this Rourke woman had started interfering!

Judith turned her face to the window, blinking away sudden tears. Trinity College disappeared into a watery blur as they swept past, people looking at the elegant cars, waving at the happy couple.

She should have realised what was happening.

It had all started innocently enough. Frances Rourke-Heffernan had been one of her mother's closest friends. Although there was an age difference of nearly fifteen years between the two women, they went everywhere together, and sometimes people had even mistaken Frankie for Margaret Meredith's daughter. The two women had a lot in common: they were from similar backgrounds, they shared common interests and had both competed in showjumping competitions at international level. The Rourke-Heffernan stables were amongst the biggest in Ireland, and the two women had often gone riding together, though neither of them had continued jumping professionally.

They had been riding when the accident happened.

Judith squeezed her eyes shut, biting her lips to prevent the tears from spoiling her make-up. She had come close to crying on several occasions today, especially when she had heard her father say, 'I do,' and that horrible woman repeating, 'I do,' and then the kiss. But she had made a promise to herself that she wasn't going to cry today.

She had been in boarding school in the south of England when she had learned the news of her mother's death. It had been a Wednesday afternoon, and she'd been called out in the middle of art class, and told to go to the headmistress's office. Walking down the long polished corridor, she remembered desperately trying to work out what she had done wrong over the previous couple of days. But the moment she had seen her father sitting there, with the deep shadows under his eyes, stubble on his chin, the knot of his tie loose, she knew that something was desperately wrong.

The headmistress had excused herself and left the room, and then her father had taken her onto his knee—

something he hadn't done since she was a very small child—
and explained to her that he had just flown in from Dublin.
His voice was very soft as he told her that there had been a
riding accident. Her mother had been thrown from her
horse. By the time the doctor had been called, and the
ambulance had taken her to hospital, she had been uncon-
scious. Margaret Meredith had died quite peacefully in her
sleep, never regaining consciousness.

And Frances Rourke-Heffernan had been with her. She
had been with her when she had the accident; with her
when she died. She'd been there by Maxwell's side at the
funeral, and then the tall, elegant blonde had become a
regular visitor to the Meredith household in the weeks and
months following Margaret's death.

Judith realised that the process leading up to today had
probably begun then, but she had been too young, too
immature to realise what was happening. Maxwell Meredith
was wealthy, handsome and powerful: he would be quite a
catch for any woman, even one fifteen years his junior.

They had broken the news to her six months ago. The
three of them had been out to dinner together, and during
dessert, her father had simply said, without warning, 'Frankie
and I are going to get married.' While she had stared at him
in horror, the woman had leaned across the table, bright blue
eyes blinking innocently, and she had smiled at Judith. 'I'm
not even going to try to replace Margaret—no-one could do
that—but I hope we'll be friends.'

Judith hadn't said anything then. She had simply smiled,
excused herself from the table . . . and been violently sick
in the toilets.

There was no way she would ever be friends with the
woman. Not if she was the last person left on this world.
That woman had stolen her father away from her, stolen her
mother's memory away from him.

And how could he? How could he?

Judith had thought that he loved her mother: they always seemed so happy together. But if he had loved her, then he wouldn't be getting married so soon after her death, would he? No, he had obviously been waiting for her to die . . . he had probably even been glad that she had died!

The white Rolls Royce pulled up in front of the Shelbourne Hotel. Judith watched as the uniformed doorman opened the door, reaching in with his gloved hand for the new Mrs Rourke-Heffernan Meredith . . . or was she going to call herself Mrs Rourke Meredith or Heffernan-Meredith or simply Mrs Meredith? The latter, Judith decided. The woman had taken everything else belonging to her mother; she might as well complete the job and take her name as well.

The limousine carrying Judith, her brother Morgan and his tiny wife Peggy pulled in down the street. Cars driving around Stephen's Green blared their horns in salute. Everyone was smiling, laughing—even strangers in the street wishing the couple every happiness—everyone except Judith. The tall, blonde-haired, brown-eyed young woman stood well back in the crowd, watching the bride and groom intently as they posed in front of the hotel's ornate canopy while more photographs were taken. In that moment she hated them both for what they had done, hated them with an intensity that she didn't know she possessed. She watched while her father stood up on his toes, looking around, finally catching sight of her in the crowd, calling her forward, positioning her between Frankie and himself while the photographer called for a 'family shot', and Judith, looking up at the pretty smiling woman, decided that she didn't want to be a member of any family this woman was a part of. They all turned then and trooped through the hotel foyer, cameras flashing, conversation buzzing, the sounds high-pitched and brittle, broken by laughter.

Judith trailed along behind almost reluctantly, the smile on her face not quite a grimace.

The meal was gorgeous, but went on for ever, and then there were the speeches, and they seemed to go on even longer. Judith ate little, barely tasting the food, and didn't even bother to listen to the speeches until her father stood up. He was a superb public speaker and people began laughing and smiling almost immediately, as he told joke after joke about the preparations for the wedding. He thanked everyone, and then invited the guests to raise their glasses in a toast to all those who had helped . . . his new mother- and father-in-law, his sister and brothers-in-law. Judith's face burned bright red when he proposed a toast to her, and she had to sit while everyone stood and raised their glasses to her. 'For my own Judy, whom I'll never be able to thank for all the help she gave me when I needed it. I only hope I'll be there if she ever needs me.'

When he proposed a toast to Margaret, a complete silence fell over the room and the glasses were raised silently. 'I know Margaret is here today in spirit; I know she would approve.'

Judith Meredith lowered her head, biting down hard on the soft flesh inside her cheeks to keep the tears away.

There was no way her mother would approve!

Later, she supposed that the idea had been buzzing around in the back of her mind for ages, but when the party moved out of the dining-room and into the ballroom, when the crowd was mingling together and it was easy to stand well back and get lost amongst all the people, the whole plan just seemed to come together, all neat and complete.

Maxwell Meredith had taken two double rooms on the top floor of the hotel; one for himself and his new bride and the other for Judith, the bridesmaid, and Frankie's sister, Sylvia, the matron-of-honour, where they could change into their evening clothes.

Judith hung back until she saw her father and his new bride leave the room arm in arm, followed, a few moments later, by the matron-of-honour. She glanced at her tiny wristwatch. It was eight o'clock. They would change and be back down in about an hour. By then, most of the people who hadn't been guests at the wedding meal, but who had been invited to the party afterwards, would have arrived, bringing the numbers up to nearly four hundred. That's when she'd act.

Judith spent the next hour hurrying from one side of the room to the other, dodging various aunts and uncles. She carried two glasses of orange juice with her, so that if she was stopped she could say she was just bringing this drink over to so-and-so.

Finally, just when she was beginning to think that her parents—no, her father and her step-mother—would never reappear, there was a round of applause as they entered the room. She had done something to her hair and was now wearing a dress that looked like something from a bad American soap opera, while her father was elegant in a charcoal grey double-breasted suit. Sylvia hovered behind the couple, wearing a dress that might have looked pretty on a woman ten years younger and two stone lighter.

Judith waited until the crowd had swallowed up her father and step-mother and then slid through the crowd until she was beside her new step-aunt.

'We were looking everywhere for you,' the small, stout woman rounded on Judith. 'You should change.'

'I met some friends,' Judith lied. 'I didn't realise that time had slipped away.'

'Well, I'm so glad you're enjoying yourself. They make such a lovely couple, don't they?'

'Gorgeous,' Judith said, unable to keep the sarcasm from her voice.

Sylvia looked at her sharply.

'If you give me the key to the room, I'll go and change,' Judith continued, turning away to look around the room, waving at no-one in particular.

Her step-aunt handed her the plastic-tagged key. 'Try not to be too long, dear; it looks like the party is just beginning to hot up. We were thinking of going along to a nightclub afterwards,' she added.

'I think I'm a bit too young for a nightclub,' Judith mumbled.

Sylvia leaned forward and whispered conspiratorially, 'Well, it's supposed to be a surprise for Frankie, but your father has booked out one of the clubs in Baggot Street. It'll be just for us. What do you think of that?'

'I can't wait.' She looked at the woman, who was almost old enough to be her mother, and smiled again. 'I had better go and change then, hadn't I?'

After the noise and confusion of the ballroom, the rest of the hotel seemed deathly quiet. She rustled down the corridors, holding her dress up, humming softly to herself as she counted the numbers on the doors. She stopped when she realised she was humming 'Here Comes the Bride'.

Her father had taken two interconnecting rooms. The first one was a mess. The suitcases that had been sent over the night before lay open on the beds, and clothes were scattered everywhere. For a moment Judith thought they had been burgled, but as she walked around, she noticed that the wedding dress—over three thousand pounds worth—lay crumpled on the floor where it had been dropped, while her father's eight hundred pound suit was neatly folded across the back of a chair. There was a bottle of champagne in an ice bucket at the end of the bed with two glasses on the table beside it, one of them with a bright red lipstick stain around the rim.

In the adjoining room, Sylvia's lavender dress was tossed across the end of the bed, and the contents of her suitcase scattered across the duvet. Judith looked into the suitcase, wondering why the woman had brought three complete changes of clothes: surely she had known what she was going to change into?

Struggling with the zip of her own dress, she crossed to where her small suitcase had been laid on the second bed. She had brought two changes of clothing with her: a simple, but elegant, party dress with a low bodice and a deep-cut back that was vaguely Spanish in appearance, and also her dancing clothes . . . because she had known that her father was booking the nightclub in Baggot Street! She decided on her dancing clothes, not only because they were more comfortable, but because they were also more practical. She dressed quickly, terrified now that someone would come up to the room. Then she stood in front of the mirrored wardrobe to look at herself.

She was fifteen years old, tall, blonde-haired, with huge brown eyes that were just a little shortsighted, set into a rather long, oval face. Fifteen hundred pounds of dental work had ensured that her teeth were perfect. She stuck her hands in the pockets of her stone-washed jeans and tried to be critical about herself. With the make-up, the high-necked ruffled blouse, the jeans with the matching denim jacket and the low brown boots, she decided she looked about seventeen. It would do; it would have to.

She emptied the contents of her purse onto the bed. She had thirty pounds in cash, a few bits of make-up and a comb. She stuck the comb in her back pocket and distributed the money into her various pockets. Lipstick, eye-shadow, foundation cream and blusher went into the inside pockets. She was going to need that make-up to add years to her face.

Fifteen minutes later, Judith Meredith walked out of the front door of the Shelbourne Hotel and turned right, heading towards Grafton Street. She had no real idea where she was going or what she was going to do. She needed time to herself to think, time to work out a few things.

She had come to one conclusion though: she didn't think there was room for her now in her father's life.

2

The city looked different at night. Even Grafton Street, one of the few streets with which she was familiar, looked completely changed.

Judith Meredith had led a very sheltered life that had always been cushioned by her parents' wealth. She went to boarding school in England and only came over to Ireland during the holidays. She would spend a day or two in Ireland before they flew off on a summer or winter vacation, so she actually saw very little of the country she'd been born in. On the few occasions when she had come in to the city, it had always been in the company of her parents, and even then they usually shopped around Grafton Street, although they occasionally ventured down into O'Connell Street and Henry Street. During term, when she wanted or needed something, she would write to her father at the London office, and a few days later whatever she'd asked for would arrive in the post.

She was fifteen years old—and she was still treated as if she was a child. It was only on occasions like this, when she suddenly discovered how little she knew, that the realisation struck home. Judith shivered, digging her hands into her pockets. The night wasn't cold—far from it—but she suddenly felt very alone, very lost in the big city.

She continued down Grafton Street until she reached College Green, where she stopped to catch her breath and take her bearings. She hadn't wanted to stop close to the hotel, just in case someone had seen her leave and had come after her.

But now she needed time to think.

She continued around by Trinity College and crossed into Westmoreland Street, heading for O'Connell Bridge.

It was a mild, warm evening and the streets were crowded, couples walking arm-in-arm, people strolling along, children weaving in around the crowd, hassled mothers chasing them. There were long queues at the bus stops in Westmoreland Street, and looking at them, Judith suddenly realised she had never been on a bus in her life.

She crossed O'Connell Bridge and stopped, looking up and down the quays, and then peering down into O'Connell Street. There was still time to go back to the hotel.

She shook her head angrily, surprising a young couple who were standing beside her, waiting to cross onto Bachelor's Walk. The lights changed and they hurried across, laughing quietly together. Judith knew they were laughing at her. Annoyed with herself, she turned to the left and hurried up the quays.

She needed time to think!

And she wasn't going to be able to do it strolling around the streets. She'd find a café, buy a cup of tea and sit down and work out her options. She glanced at her wristwatch: twenty to ten. She wondered how much longer she had before it was discovered that she was missing from the hotel.

And once they discovered, would they care?

Judith turned right at the Ha'penny Bridge into Liffey Street. There were a couple of cafés on either side of the street, and she chose the first one. She opened the door and stepped into the warm, slightly stale smell of cooking oil, mingled with the sharper tang of vinegar. There were perhaps half a dozen people present in the long narrow room and they all looked up as she entered.

A stout, pleasant-faced woman looked up as Judith approached the plastic topped counter. 'Yes, luv?'

'Tea, please.'

'Mug or a pot?'

'Oh. Ahem . . . a mug please.' She didn't know how big a pot was, and she also realised she was going to have to be careful with her money now.

The woman pushed across a steaming mug of dark tea. Judith was surprised to discover that the tea bag was still in the cup. She handed across a five-pound note, not knowing how much it was going to cost: she spent her allowance on make-up, small items of clothes, records, videos, costume jewellery. The woman gave her £4.60 change.

Judith took a spoon from the tray by the counter and slid into a corner seat. She added milk from a metal jug on the table, reached for a sachet of sugar and then stirred her tea. Staring deep into the murky liquid, she wondered what she was going to do. What was she doing, for goodness sake?

She was running away, that's what she was doing.

O.K. But where was she going?

Sipping the hot tea, wincing as it stung at her palate, she considered the possibilities. If she was running away, she had to have somewhere to run to, didn't she? She might be very naive in many ways because she'd led a sheltered life, but she still had a very good idea what happened to young women on the streets.

So she needed to go somewhere. A friend . . . a relative . . . Aunt Jean!

A slow smile curled her thin lips upwards. Jean Ashe was her late mother's sister. She hadn't attended the wedding, and she had made her dislike of Frankie quite obvious: she hadn't even sent a wedding present. Aunt Jean usually spent the summers in her house just outside Salthill, overlooking Galway Bay. She could go there, couldn't she? She could stay with Jean until she worked out her long-term plans . . .

Judith looked up as the three young men crowded her table. They were all aged between thirteen and sixteen. Two slid into the seat directly across from her, while the third sat down beside her, effectively trapping her in the booth.

'Hello.' The one directly across from her smiled, showing broken, dirty teeth.

'We thought you looked lonely,' his companion added. He was tall and wiry, face spotted with pimples.

'We thought you'd like a little company,' the one beside her said, with a thin smile. His hair, thick with grease or gel, was swept back off his face. All three were dressed in black jeans and black t-shirts advertising various heavy metal bands.

'Please go away,' Judith said loudly, wrapping her hands around her mug.

'Please go away,' the young man beside her mimicked. 'My, hasn't she got a posh accent.'

'Bit posh for here,' the boy sitting across from her said, licking his lips slowly and deliberately.

'Aaah, I think she's playing hard to get,' his friend added. 'Else why would she come in here in the first place?'

'Leave me alone.' She straightened in the chair and looked at the youth sitting beside her. 'Excuse me, I want to go.'

He looked at his two friends and grinned, but didn't move.

'I said I want to leave.' She looked up at the counter, but the woman was nowhere to be seen.

'But we don't want you to leave.'

'What's your name, darling?'

'Bet it's a nice name. A posh name.'

'I'll scream,' she threatened, half rising to her feet. She could feel the tears starting to come, but she was determined not to cry in front of these three hooligans.

The one sitting beside her—who seemed to be the leader—put his hand on her arm and pressed her back into the seat. Although he was still smiling, his eyes were cold and hard. 'Oh, I wouldn't scream if I were you,' he murmured.

Judith looked down at the hand on her arm. The finger-nails were chewed to the quick, and the tips of his fingers were brown from cigarettes. She realised now that she was in trouble. She took a deep breath to calm herself; all she had to do was to stay calm and wait until the woman came back to the counter, and then she'd scream. They'd go then.

And if they didn't?

Judith saw him before any of the others. He was sitting on the other side of the aisle, lounging back against the wall, a mug of tea in one hand, the other stretched out across the back of the chair. He finished his tea, slid out of the seat and approached her table. Her heart sank: here was another one!

'Let the young lady go.'

Everyone turned to look at the tall young man who had rested both fists on the table and was leaning forward, staring intently at the youth sitting beside Judith.

'You looking for some sort of trouble?' the young man sitting across from her asked loudly, his eyes beginning to glitter with a dangerous excitement.

'Stop hassling the lady, let her go, and there'll be no trouble.' He spoke in a strange, almost rural accent.

'And who's going to give us any trouble. You?' the young man sitting beside her sneered, his right hand beginning to slide into his pocket.

'You better believe it,' the tall young man said very quietly. And then his hand shot out, trapping the other youth's hand in his pocket. 'You better not have anything in your hand when you take it out of your pocket,' he said with a smile that was frightening.

The youth sitting across from Judith suddenly pointed to the stranger's hand, drawing everyone's attention to the large black spider tattooed onto the skin between his thumb and forefinger.

'You're Spider!' he whispered, making it sound like an accusation.

Judith saw the colour change in the gang leader's face. He twisted his head to look at the large hand that was crushing his own, and then he looked up into the young man's eyes. 'You're Spider?

'You know me?' the young man asked, his eyes never leaving the leader's face.

'Yea, yea. Look, we didn't know she was with you. Right. I mean . . . Look. Sorry. We're going.'

Spider stepped back and allowed the young man to squeeze past him. His two friends quickly slid out of the seat and all three hurried towards the door without looking back. When the door had closed behind them, Spider walked around the counter, and returned a few moments later with two cups. He slid into the seat across from Judith and pushed the fresh cup of tea over in front of her.

'You all right?'

She nodded. 'I am. Thank you.'

He jerked his head in the direction of the door. 'On their own they're harmless, but put them together and they get mean and ugly.'

Judith sipped her tea, looking at the young man. She found it difficult to put an age on him. Twenty maybe? His face was long and narrow, with skin so deeply tanned that she knew he must spend a lot of time in the open air, and his eyes were so dark they looked black—she'd never met anyone with black eyes before. His hair was thick and black, dragged back off his face into a tiny pony tail. He wore blue jeans so faded they were almost white, a white t-shirt that was in need of a wash and a black leather motor-cycle jacket that was beginning to crack and fray. There was a small hooped earring in his left ear.

'I'm sorry,' she said, realising that he was talking to her

'I was wondering what you're doing here. Are you waiting for someone?'

'Yes,' she said immediately, and then shook her head. 'No, I'm not.'

'Lost?'

She shook her head again.

Spider sat back and sipped his tea, looking at her over the rim of his cup.

Judith looked past him. She thought she could see one of the gang staring in through the window.

'They'll hang around for a while maybe,' he said without turning around. 'And then they'll get bored.'

'Thanks again,' she smiled. 'I thought they were just messing at first.' She lifted her cup and her fingers were shaking. 'They frightened me,' she admitted. 'Why do they call you Spider?' she asked suddenly.

He grinned and showed her the tattoo again.

'I'm Judith . . . I mean my name is Judith.'

'Judith,' he said, pronouncing it joo-dit. 'It's a nice name,' he nodded. He looked at her for a few moments, and then asked, 'Are you in trouble?'

'I don't know,' she murmured. 'I'm running away . . . or at least, I'm trying to.' She smiled and glanced at her watch. 'Look at me; I ran away about half an hour ago, and already I'm in trouble.'

'Dressed like you are, looking like you, in a place like this, you're bound to attract attention.'

'What do you mean?' She had deliberately worn her jeans, hoping she would blend in more easily.

'Your clothes are too new, it's obvious you don't wear them all the time. Your make-up is very good, but it draws attention to your face, and your hair is beautiful. If you want to try and survive on the streets or stay out of trouble, you should dress and look, even walk, so as not to attract attention.'

'You sound as if you're speaking from experience,' she said with a smile.

'I am.'

Judith looked up in alarm as the door opened, but it was only a young couple pushing a buggy.

'Are you in trouble with the police?' Spider asked
'No.'

'Why are you running away?'

'It's a long story,' she sighed.

He nodded slightly. 'But in the end the reasons are usually the same.'

Judith looked at him quickly.

'I ran away myself a couple of times,' he admitted. 'Where are you headed?'

'Galway. I've an aunt there.'

'I'm going to Galway too,' he said, finishing his tea. 'This is Galway Race Week. Some of my family will be there. I'm going to meet them.' He paused and added, 'You're welcome to come with me, if you like.'

His offer took her by surprise. On the surface he looked very like the three thugs who had terrorised her, but even they had been frightened of him, so what did that make him? She shook her head, smiling slightly. 'I was going to get the train . . .'

'That'd be quicker. But if someone was looking for you, that's one of the first things they'd think of. Do you know where the station is?'

She was about to lie, but then she shook her head. 'I don't know Dublin very well at all.'

'I can show you,' he said, standing up.

'Thank you.'

The three thugs were waiting outside the café, lounging up against a wall across the narrow street. They came to attention when Spider and Judith stepped out into the street.

'Hey . . . you!' the leader called.

Spider swore under his breath. He reached into the back pocket of his jeans and pulled out a key. 'Can you drive?' he muttered.

'I haven't got a licence.'

'Can you drive?'

'Well . . . yes.'

'There's a blue Toyota van in the lane to your left. Bring it around here as fast as you can. Don't forget to take the lock off the passenger door.'

Judith's heart was pounding and her mouth was dry. 'What about you?'

'I'm going to have a few words with our friends here. Now go . . . go!' He pushed her away from him and strode across the street, pushing up the sleeves of his leather jacket. He walked right up to the leader, and poked his shoulder with a straight forefinger. 'Have you got a problem with me?'

Judith raced down the narrow side street, her boots sliding on the cobbles. The blue Toyota was parked on a double yellow line in front of a gate that said, 'No Parking'. As she fumbled with the key in the lock she heard shouts from the street behind her. Climbing up into the driver's seat, she was surprised to find how high up she was. She had driven her father's Mercedes and her mother's Volvo on a couple of occasions, but always only on quiet country roads or in empty car parks. And the dashboard of the van bore no resemblance to either of those cars. There was no gear-stick for a start, and the pedals were a long way down.

The shouting had now got louder and she could see people beginning to gather.

Think. Think. *Think.*

All cars were basically the same, therefore there had to be a gear-stick . . . She touched a lever sticking out behind the steering wheel. What did this do? On the cars she had driven, a similar stick controlled the windscreen wipers or the lights, but she could see the switches here that controlled both. Therefore . . .

Judith trod heavily on the clutch and moved the stick, and then laughed aloud in triumph: it *was* the gear-lever. Turning the key in the ignition, she pressed too heavily on the accelerator and the engine roared to life. Manoeuvring the gears with difficulty, she sent the van jerking forward before she managed to control it. With the wheels squealing on the cobbles, she sent the van careering down the Lotts and around into Lower Liffey Street.

And almost ran over Spider.

She arrived in time to see him pick up the smallest of the three louts and throw him at the other two. The three of them went down in a bundle of arms and legs.

Spider snatched at the passenger door, but she had forgotten to open it. He hammered on the window. As she leaned over to unlock it, the engine cut out.

And now there were police running around from Abbey Street.

Spider scrambled into the van. 'Back up, back up!' he panted

'I can't work the gears.'

'I'll change gear—you just drive. Now reverse!'

Judith sent the van screeching backwards, scattering curious onlookers in every direction. When she'd passed the entrance to the laneway—the Lotts—Spider slammed the van into first gear and Judith hauled it around the corner. As they raced down the narrow lane, Spider called, 'Change gear,' and she stood on the clutch while he manoeuvred the gears. At the bottom of the lane, they turned to the right, down an even narrower lane, and then to the left, out onto Bachelor's Walk. The traffic lights were with them and they turned to the right across O'Connell Bridge into D'Olier street. As they turned into College Street, the lights changed, and Spider sat back into his seat. When Judith glanced at him, she found he was grinning broadly. There was a bruise on his chin and strands of hair were falling across his forehead. 'You can drive,' he complimented her.

'Thank you. It's just that I've never driven a van with gears like this.'

'You didn't have to come back for me,' he said seriously, watching as she deftly manoeuvred the van into first gear and pulled away smoothly, turning right into Westmoreland Street. 'You're a quick learner too,' he added.

'Did you think I wouldn't come back?'

He shrugged. 'It was a possibility.'

'But you helped me. I didn't even think about not coming back.' And it was true, she realised, she hadn't even stopped to consider it. 'I was afraid you were going to get hurt.'

Spider laughed aloud, and then he pointed to the left. 'We turn here, we're going up the quays. There were only three of them,' he continued, and Judith wasn't sure if he was joking or not. 'No, they weren't the problem. The police would have been the problem,' he added with a sigh.

Judith glanced at him quickly. He was sitting back in the seat, with his head tilted back, eyes closed. 'Are you in trouble with the police?' she asked, asking him the same question he had asked her earlier.

'Not at the moment. Not for anything in particular. But then, people like me are always in trouble with the police.' He suddenly straightened and pointed off to the left. 'Heuston Station is in here. That's where you'll get the train to Galway.'

All her life Judith Meredith's decisions had been made for her. Tonight, she had actually made a decision—an important decision—for herself. She had taken control of her own life and run away. She was about to make another equally important decision.

'Is that offer to take me to Galway still open?' she asked.

3

'What do you mean she's not here?' Maxwell Meredith rounded on Sylvia.

'I've looked everywhere for her. I can't find her in the hotel.'

The tall, elegant man ran his fingers through his carefully groomed hair. 'When did you last see her?' he demanded loudly. Silence was gradually falling over the wedding guests as they realised that something was wrong.

'When I gave her the key to the room. She was going to change.'

'Have you been up there?'

'Well, I can't really,' she blinked. 'She didn't give me back the key.'

'What time was that?'

'Oh, about nine, something like that.'

'And you haven't seen her since then?'

The stout woman shook her head, her large eyes suddenly swimming in unshed tears.

Maxwell glanced at his watch. It was close to eleven now. He looked at his new wife and she nodded slightly, pointing upwards.

'I'll come with you,' he muttered.

'She didn't look too happy today,' Frankie murmured, as they hurried from the ballroom.

'I know. She's probably off sulking somewhere. For all we know she could have fallen asleep upstairs.'

They made their way up through the hotel in virtual silence. The top floor was deserted, and after the heat and cigarette fumes of the ballroom, the air smelt fresh and clean. Maxwell knocked loudly on the pale cream-coloured door of Judith's room. He waited a moment before finally using his own key to gain admittance.

Maxwell moved quickly into the adjoining room, stopping when he saw that Judith wasn't there. He had fully expected to find her asleep on the bed. Frankie brushed past him and lifted the bridesmaid's dress off the end of the bed. And then she spotted the girl's purse which had been left on the bed. When she looked at her husband, her eyes were wide with fright.

Maxwell took a deep breath. 'I'm calling the manager. I want this hotel searched from top to bottom. If she's not here, I'm phoning the police!'

Sunday 29th July

4

Judith awoke with a start, eyes blinking rapidly. She sat up straight abruptly, and then groaned aloud as tired, cramped muscles protested. She felt as stiff as a board. She looked around, confused and disorientated, but then in a rush, the events of the past few hours flooded back.

She was in Spider's van on the road to Galway!

But where was Spider? Why had they stopped? Had something happened?

She raised her hand to massage her stiff neck muscles and the blanket that had been wrapped around her fell away. She didn't remember falling asleep. She looked at her watch: it was ten past five . . . in the morning! Leaning forward, she ran her hand down the fogged-up windscreen. The dawn was grey and gritty outside the window. They were parked on the side of the road, beneath the shelter of some trees . . . and then she realised what had woken her: it was the water dripping from the branches overhead onto the metal roof of the van.

But where was Spider?

He had instructed her to drive into the Phoenix Park where they had changed positions, and he had taken over the driving. They hadn't spoken much in the next hour or so. He seemed intent on leaving the city as quickly as possible, and she realised that the idea of the police had frightened him far more than the three toughs. Her last memory was of him driving—surprisingly slowly, she thought—with the radio turned down low to 2FM.

There was a curious scrabbling sound behind her and she twisted stiffly in the seat to look into the back of the van. Spider was sleeping on the floor, bundled up in a soiled sleeping bag. There were a few items of clothing scattered around the van, a sagging armchair, a small portable television and radio, a primus stove, and Judith suddenly realised that this was where he lived!

The young man murmured in his sleep, and Judith could see that his eyeballs were moving rapidly behind his closed eyelids. She wondered what he was dreaming about. Sleep had erased a lot of the lines from his face. The lines that creased his forehead, tightened the skin around his eyes and mouth, making him seem older, were gone. When she first saw him she thought he was around twenty, but looking at him now, she decided he looked closer to seventeen.

She looked around the back of the van again as the realisation sunk in that he was seventeen years old and he lived out of the back of a van . . .

Spider's eyes flickered open and he sat up smoothly, bright-eyed and alert. He ran his hands through his hair, drawing it back off his face while he watched her.

His intense scrutiny was unnerving and Judith looked away.

'Good morning,' she murmured.

'Yea.' Spider drew his legs up and slid out of the sleeping bag. He stretched, his fingertips touching the sides of the van, his head brushing the roof. Leaning over the driver's seat, he peered out through the fogged-up windows. 'What time is it? Feels early!'

'Just after five.'

He nodded. 'You hungry?'

She nodded.

'You have a choice: you can have tea or you can have tea.'

'I'll have tea,' she smiled. She swivelled around in the seat to watch him light up the primus stove and fill a small blackened kettle with water from a bottle.

'Conditions here are probably not what you're used to,' he said with a grin. 'Oh, and if you're looking for a toilet—there isn't one. They don't fit them to this model van. But don't worry, we'll head into Maynooth in a couple of hours, and we'll find you a loo there.'

'I'm fine,' she murmured, vaguely embarrassed to hear him speak so frankly about toilets; it wasn't the sort of thing people she knew spoke of. It wasn't polite. 'When will we get to Galway?' she asked, changing the subject.

'Later today, before noon certainly.'

'I really appreciate what you're doing . . . .'

Spider shook his head. 'Don't worry about it.' He was concentrating on the primus. 'You've got to be careful of these,' he muttered. 'Really should be doing it outside.'

'Do you live here?' Judith asked. 'I mean, in the van?

'Yea. Not bad, is it?' He grinned at her startled expression. 'Well, I'm sure it's not what you're used to. You've probably got a bedroom that's bigger than this.' He shrugged, adding a single tea bag to the bubbling water. 'But I don't need very much more than this. I've got everything I want right here.'

She nodded, surprised by his attitude. 'But if anything should happen to the van . . . ?'

'And if anything should happen to your house . . . ?' He reached into a cardboard box, took out a dusty cup, and stood it alongside a chipped and battered enamel mug that had seen a lot of use. 'There's not a lot of difference really . . .' He paused and considered. 'Well there is, I suppose. If anything happens to your house, you'll lose a lot of personal things, little bits of memories. When you live on the streets, or when you're constantly travelling, you learn to do one of two things: either you don't collect bits and pieces, or you carry them around with you.' He looked up. 'Milk? Sugar?'

'Milk and sugar, please.'

Spider handed her the tea and then climbed into the front seat with his own mug. He rolled down the window slightly and breathed deeply. The air was sharp and damp and cold.

Judith wrapped her hands around her mug and sipped the scalding liquid. She'd had her doubts when she'd seen how he made it—but it tasted delicious. She could feel it working its way into her stomach. 'And what do you do?' she asked.

He looked at her blankly.

'I mean, do you collect bits and pieces?'

Spider tapped the side of his head with a long forefinger. 'Only in here.'

They drank their tea in silence, allowing the warm liquid to heat them up.

'This is the first time you've run away,' Spider said suddenly.

It wasn't a question, but Judith still answered him. 'Yes. How did you know?' And then she grinned. 'Do I look that naive?'

He nodded. 'No, it's not just that . . . it's difficult to explain, but when you've lived on the streets for a while, you develop a look, an attitude, a wariness. You haven't got that look yet. And besides, you trusted me too easily,' he laughed. 'Do you want to tell me why you ran away? I'll understand if you don't,' he added quickly.

Judith leaned forward and rubbed her hand down the glass, clearing a space in it for her to look out into the grey morning. To the east the horizon was already turning bright with the sunrise.

'Are your parents alive, Spider?' she asked quietly.

'My father's alive; my mother died a little while back.'

'Just like me,' she muttered. 'Did you like them?'

The young man glanced at her sharply, frowning.

Judith saw the look of surprise on his face. 'I know. You're not supposed to like your parents, you're supposed to love them without thinking about it. You just accept it.' She swivelled around in the seat to face him, her large brown eyes wide and serious. 'But did your parents ever do anything that made you . . . made you dislike them, maybe even hate them?'

Spider watched her face, wondering what she was leading up to. He knew that if he spoke now he would interrupt her train of thought, and he sensed that this was probably the first time she had ever seriously considered her feelings. Judith turned away to stare straight ahead through the moisture-streaked window.

'My mother died just over two years ago in a riding accident. Yesterday, my father married her best friend.'

'You don't like the woman?' Spider murmured.

'No! Why did Dad have to marry her. Why why *why*!'

'Maybe because he loved her,' Spider suggested.

'He loved my mother—or at least he said he did.'

'And now your mother is dead,' Spider said, attempting to understand her anger. 'Why can't he love someone else? Isn't it possible to love more than one person at any one time?'

'But this woman is awful. She's just . . . so . . . so empty. So stupid. I'm sure she tricked him into marrying her!'

'Do you love your father?' Spider asked suddenly, surprising her.

'Of course!' She sounded almost insulted that he would have suggested otherwise.

'Do you think he'd ever make a mistake?'

'No,' she shook her head without hesitation.

'But you think he was foolish enough to fall into this rather stupid woman's trap!'

Judith turned to look at Spider. He glanced sidelong at her and winked. 'Couldn't be that you simply don't like this woman and that's all there is to it?'

'She's trying to take the place of my mother.'

'But she can't do that if you don't let her.'

'She'll try. Before the wedding she said we were going to be great friends.'

'What's wrong with that?'

'It was the way she said it!'

Spider nodded, without saying anything. He eventually broke the long silence that followed. 'Do you think your father loves this woman?'

'Yes. No. I don't know. I suppose so.'

'If I was you, I'd be glad that he's been lucky enough to find another person to love.' Judith turned to stare at him. But before she could reply, Spider turned the key in the ignition. The motor whined, caught and died, whined again and finally coughed into life.

'Let's go to Galway,' he suggested.

Maxwell Meredith replaced the phone and turned to look at Frankie. 'Nothing.'

'You've tried everyone?' the tall, blonde-haired woman asked.

'Everyone,' he said tiredly. He sat down on the edge of the bed and buried his head in his hands. Frankie came and sat beside him, wrapping her arms around his shoulders. 'Do you think she's run away, Maxwell?' she whispered.

'Where would she run to? She's nowhere to go. She didn't want me to get married,' he said numbly.

'I would never have gone ahead if I'd known that this was going to happen,' Frankie said quietly. 'Your happiness means too much to me. We could have waited.'

'That's if she has run away,' Maxwell continued, not looking at his wife, continuing his train of thought.

'What do you mean?'

Maxwell looked into his wife's eyes. 'What are we going to do if she's been kidnapped!'

They drove out of Maynooth a little after nine, having bought some fresh fruit and cans of soft drinks in a tiny shop just off the main street.

On the long road between Kilcock and Enfield, the Toyota began to sputter, the engine coughing and cutting out. They were about a mile outside Enfield when it finally cut out completely and simply refused to start up again.

Spider put the van into neutral and allowed it to coast to the side of the road.

'What's wrong?' Judith asked when he'd stopped swearing.

'I meant to get it seen to in Dublin,' he muttered.

'What's wrong?' Judith demanded again.

'Nothing's wrong. Well, nothing much,' he added. 'Let's go and see if we can get someone to give us a tow.' He looked at her and shrugged ruefully. 'I'm afraid you won't be arriving in Galway today.'

Inspector Maurice Doyle was a bulky soft-spoken man in his late fifties. He sat on the long leather sofa in the enormous sitting-room that looked out over Killiney Bay and watched the couple sitting across from him. He'd read the case reports before he'd come over; he knew they'd been married only yesterday and should be in Hawaii on their honeymoon by now. He also knew that their combined wealth must make them amongst the richest couples in Ireland. He coughed into his hand, realising that they were expecting him to say something. His main intention now was to reassure them, keep them calm.

'From what you have told me, my immediate reaction is that the girl has simply run away because she was upset about the wedding. It happens,' he shrugged. 'If it's a spur of the moment thing, girls like this usually go to their nearest friend, spend the night there and come back in the morning, suitably ashamed. I think it's significant that Judith didn't go to any of her friends.'

'Why is it significant, inspector?' Frankie asked.

'It might mean that she's been planning this for a while, ma'am.'

'I phoned everyone,' Maxwell said.

'Has she a boyfriend?' Inspector Doyle asked.

Maxwell shook his head.

'You're sure?'

'I'm sure.'

The inspector smiled kindly. 'Well, let me ask you the question in another way. Has she any male friends, someone she hangs around with, talks about, goes to town with, swaps records or books with? Maybe the brother of one of her girl friends? Just because you think she doesn't have a boyfriend, doesn't mean she hasn't a boyfriend.'

'There's no-one to the best of my knowledge,' Maxwell said. 'She goes to boarding school in England. She's only over here on holidays. And besides, I'm not even sure if she's even started thinking about boys yet. She's led a very sheltered life.' He looked the inspector in the eye. 'You haven't said anything about the alternative.'

The inspector nodded again. 'Yes, there is an alternative that you should be aware of . . .'

'You think she might have been kidnapped?'

'It is possible, Mr Meredith. Although, if she had been kidnapped, you should have heard something already or, at the very least, you will hear something today.' He stood up and straightened his uniform. 'If you have a recent picture of your daughter, I will see that it is circulated to all our stations.'

'I would prefer if this didn't get into the news,' Maxwell Meredith said quickly.

'Well, there are pros and cons to that, of course, sir. If she has run away, then it makes it easier to find her, since people will know what she looks like. However, if she has been kidnapped, we would prefer if it didn't get into the papers: it makes our work a lot easier.' The tall man shook hands with Maxwell and Frankie. 'And please, get some rest and try not to worry. I'm sure all this will work out well in the end,' he added, turning and walking away before they saw the doubt in his own eyes. A fifteen-year-old girl, the daughter of one of the richest men in Ireland, goes missing . . . he was certainly expecting the worst!

5

Judith sat in the van for nearly two hours before Spider returned in a battered tow truck. He hopped out as the truck drew alongside and leaned against the door, looking up at her. He smiled sheepishly and shrugged. 'I couldn't find an open garage . . . well, I could,' he added softly, 'but they weren't too interested in coming out. I suppose they thought I was having them on or something.' He stopped and then asked, 'Are you OK?'

'Yes . . . yes, I'm fine,' she said shortly. The two hours had just dragged by, giving her time to think. Just what did she think she was doing? Where was she going to go with this young man whom she hardly knew? What had she been thinking of? All her previous excitement was beginning to drain away, and now the doubts were crowding in.

Judith climbed out of the van and stood by the side of the road while Spider and a tall thin young man with bad skin manoeuvred the truck in front of the van and hooked it up, winching the front end of the van off the road.

She would apologise to him at the first available opportunity, and then . . . and then what? Go home? Go to Galway? She shook her head in annoyance: she wished she could make a decision.

Spider came over and stood in front of her, his hands tucked into the back pockets of his jeans. 'I'm sorry . . .' he began.

'Wasn't your fault, was it? It was mine. If you hadn't saved me in Dublin, you would have had your van fixed. Am I right?'

He glanced back over his shoulder at the van, nodding slightly. 'It could be worse. There's a camp down the road; I should be able to scrounge some spare parts.'

'What sort of camp?'

'Travellers,' he said shortly, glancing at her.

She looked at him blankly.

'Travelling people,' he explained, watching her face closely. 'Itinerants, tinkers.'

Judith's eyes and mouth opened wide.

'Why, what did you think I was?' he asked curiously, lips twisting in a smile.

'I . . . I don't know. I never thought.'

'Have you been living in a box?' he asked with a grin.

'Sort of,' she admitted.

The pick-up truck driver leaned out of his window and shouted to Spider. His accent was broader than Spider's and Judith had difficulty understanding it. 'All set. Do you want a lift?'

'We'll walk, thanks all the same, Mickser.'

'Suit yourself. I'll start work on her as soon as I get back.'

'Thanks a lot.'

They watched the pick-up truck drive away in a flurry of smoke and exhaust fumes, towing the van behind it like some beached whale. When the dust had settled, they set off down the road behind it, Spider on the outside, Judith walking close to the hedgerow.

She glanced sidelong at him. 'Why did you not go in the van?'

He shrugged. 'It's a nice morning, and I love walking in the countryside . . . and I suppose I felt guilty about leaving you for so long.'

'Wasn't your fault,' she said again.

'Anyway, we wouldn't have been able to talk in the van. Mickser's all right. But he can be a bit crude, you know?'

She nodded, although she didn't really 'know'.

They walked on in silence. Spider plucked a long blade of grass from the roadside and nibbled thoughtfully on it. 'We might have to stay over in the camp,' he said eventually.

Judith looked at him, saying nothing.

'There'll be no trouble,' he assured her quickly, 'once they know you're with me.'

Judith remained silent.

He stopped and touched her elbow lightly. She turned to face him. 'You really didn't know I was a traveller, did you?'

'No,' she murmured.

'It bothers you?'

'Yes . . . no . . . I don't know.' She shrugged and looked past him, unwilling to meet his intense black eyes. 'I thought travellers were . . . well, dirty and begged on the streets.'

Spider bit back his reply.

Judith saw the sudden tightening of his expression and hurried on. 'I'm sorry. I didn't mean to insult you. It's just that . . . it's just that I don't know. I didn't know. You don't look like an itinerant.'

'And what do I look like?'

'You look like . . . like an ordinary person.'

Spider threw back his head and laughed. 'Do me a favour. Don't say that in the camp. I think I know what you mean. I suppose I'm not the usual traveller,' he admitted. 'My parents were travellers but they settled just after I was born.' He glanced sidelong at her. 'My mother had two children before me: neither of them lived. My folks wanted to give me a chance. So they gave up the road—although it was a way of life they both loved. They were always talking about it. I suppose I must have picked up on that love as a child.' He grinned, and suddenly looked years younger. 'I suppose that's why I ran away in the first place.'

'Why did you run away?' she asked, curious.

Spider shrugged. 'When I was a lad I ran away from home a couple of times. I was bored, I think. I was looking for something. It was only later, much later, after my mother died, that I realised I was trying to relive the life they had wandering the roads of Ireland.' His voice trailed away and he looked into the distance, but his eyes were unfocused, and Judith knew he was seeing another time, another place.

'I'm sorry, I didn't meant to pry . . .' she began.

'Travellers are dirty because more often than not, there isn't enough water to wash with,' he said suddenly. 'They beg because it's often the only way they have of earning money to feed their children or buy clothes. And like settled people, there are different sorts of travellers—good and bad. But people tend to lump us all together.'

'I'm sorry,' Judith said again. 'I didn't mean . . .'

Spider suddenly stopped and she turned to face him. He took several deep breaths, visibly mastering his anger. 'No, I'm the one who should be sorry. I'm not fighting with you. I'm fighting the attitudes you were brought up with. It's not your fault. I didn't mean to snap.'

'I was insensitive,' she said slowly.

'We were both wrong,' he grinned. 'Now come on, there's no point apologising, there's nothing we can do about it. Let's go find the camp. You hungry? I'm starving.'

'I'm hungry,' she nodded.

Judith could smell the camp long before she could see it. The fresh morning air was touched with the odours of smoke and cooking, hot metal, stale bodies, urine and faeces. There were dogs barking, children crying and a radio was turned up loud, the sound made tinny with the distance.

'Do you know these people?' Judith asked, sudden apprehension making her lower her voice to a whisper.

'Some,' he admitted, squinting into the distance. 'Some of them are my mother's people. My father's brother and his sons are here too, though I don't really know them. Most of them know me by reputation though,' he added wryly.

'And you can just walk in here?' she asked in astonishment.

'Of course,' he said, equally astonished. 'Travellers look after their own.'

The children appeared first. They came out from the hedges behind the couple and followed them at a safe distance, the bolder ones eventually scurrying up behind them until they were almost close enough to touch. Older children and young teenagers appeared next, all of them staring at Judith, not speaking.

She felt her heart begin to pound, her mouth grow dry. She moved slightly closer to Spider. He lowered his head. 'Don't worry. You're with me, you'll be all right.'

Spider wound his way through the caravans and parked cars, across a ground baked hard by the sun, scuffed to dust by countless feet. Scrap metal, broken cars, parts of machinery were piled up all around the edges of the camp, leaving the centre free, where a large fire had been built. Car seats had been arranged around the fire and there were a dozen people sitting on the seats. The low buzz of conversation stopped and they all turned to look at the approach of the unusual couple. Spider smiled and nodded pleasantly as he walked past. He stopped before a woman sitting a little apart from the rest and squatted down on the ground in front of her. Judith remained standing behind him.

The woman was tiny, her face incredibly lined and wrinkled, her skin coloured a deep nut brown. Her eyes were a startling shade of green, and were constantly moving, darting, watching. They locked onto Judith's face, caught her eyes and held them for a few moments before she deliberately looked away.

The old woman reached out and took Spider's large hands in hers, tiny delicate fingers moving across the lines and creases on his palms, tracking the spider tattoo on his right hand.

'Spider,' she murmured, her voice a hoarse rasp, as if her throat had been damaged once. 'I was saying to Big Mick only yesterday that we hadn't seen you for a while.'

'I was travelling, Granny,' Spider said softly.

'I know. I always ask after you. The last I heard you were in the North.'

'That was a while ago, Granny.'

'And then you went south into Cork, and I heard you'd been in Kerry too.'

Spider grinned broadly. 'Have you been keeping tabs on me, Granny?'

'Someone has to look after you,' she murmured, her face dissolving into deep lines as she smiled. 'And now you're back with us.'

'Just for a little while. Until I get the van fixed. How have you been?'

'Content,' she said shortly. She looked past Spider at Judith. 'And you've brought a friend,' she continued, making the simple statement into a question.

'She had a spot of trouble,' he said quietly. 'I'm just giving her a lift to her people in Galway.'

The old woman nodded, still staring at Judith. Spider glanced back over his shoulder and tilted his head slightly, calling her down. Judith crouched down beside him and smiled at the woman.

'This is Granny Hayes,' Spider said quietly. 'All the travellers know the Granny, and she knows all the travellers.' He looked at the woman. 'This is Judith Meredith.'

The old woman reached out with both hands and Judith, after a moment's hesitation, placed both her small, pale hands into the woman's dark, creased palms. With her eyes still locked on the girl's face, she turned her hands around and around, tracing the lines and indentations, touching the soft flesh, the pads at the base of her fingers, her short, beautifully manicured nails.

'Sorrow and anger,' she said abruptly.

'I beg your pardon?' Judith said, startled.

'I sense a great deal of sorrow and anger in you,' the old woman whispered.

Judith glanced at Spider in surprise. She attempted to pull her hands back, but the woman held onto them with surprising strength. 'Don't be frightened, child. I won't harm you. We won't harm you.' Her fingers continued moving over Judith's hands. 'Running away from a problem is not the solution,' she said. 'You must find the strength and courage to face your troubles.' She looked from Judith to Spider and then back to the girl. 'You two are going to Galway?'

Judith nodded.

Granny Hayes smiled, her gums pink and bare. 'Spider will look after you. You're lucky you met him, you know that?'

Judith nodded. 'I know.'

'He's a good lad. You can trust him.' She suddenly released the girl's hands and sat back onto the chair. 'You must be tired, hungry. Go, rest, eat. We will speak again later.'

Judith stood up and backed away from the woman. Spider too made as if he were about to stand but Granny called him forward with her finger. 'Take the girl to Galway quickly, Spider. Don't delay. She is not one of us. She can only bring us—and you, especially you—trouble.' Her fingers tightened onto his hands. 'You have never been hurt, Spider, you have never been truly hurt, not even when your mother died. But this girl can hurt you.'

'Granny . . .' he whispered.

'Listen to me, Spider. This girl can bring more trouble than even you can handle.'

6

Judith leaned up against the side of Granny Hayes'
caravan, her hands wrapped around a cup of scalding hot
tea, carefully sipping the dark liquid. She was frightened
now, truly frightened, angry with herself for her own
stupidity, for ending up in this situation. Surely she knew
enough not to take a lift from a stranger. Why, why had she
taken the lift . . . ?

Circumstances, a small voice whispered inside her.

And what was she going to do now? What could she do?
She could simply turn around and walk out of the camp.
She owed Spider nothing . . . well, that wasn't true. He had
saved her from a nasty experience, but those boys wouldn't
have done anything to her, not in a busy café in the centre
of Dublin . . . would they?

And she was no closer to Galway. In fact, she'd probably
find it harder to get to Galway now, whereas from Dublin it
was a simple train ride away. What a mess.

She wondered if anyone had missed her, or even noticed
that she had gone. Probably not, she decided, tears of self-pity
beginning to well up at the back of her eyes. She bent her
head over the metal cup and stared into its murky depths.

A shape stopped in front of her, and Judith looked up into the cold green eyes of a short, stout red-haired young woman who could have been anything from fifteen to twenty. She was holding a tiny baby in her arms. 'You all right?' she asked in a broad rural accent.

It took Judith a few moments to work out what she had said, and then she nodded. 'I am. Yes, thank you.'

'You know Spider,' the young woman said, and Judith wasn't sure whether it was a statement or a question.

Finally she nodded. 'I don't really know him. I met him yesterday,' she said and then immediately added, 'He saved me from three young men who were bothering me.'

The young woman glanced back over her shoulder to where Spider was lying flat on his back on an old door, examining the underside of the van. 'He's good that way,' she said. 'He's got a big heart.'

'Do you know him well?' Judith asked.

'Oh aye, very well,' the woman said, her lips curling in a smile, revealing bad teeth. 'All the travelling people know Spider. He's a good friend . . . and a bad enemy.' She turned back to Judith, her eyes moving slowly down the length of her body, looking at her expensive denims and boots. Her own clothes were cheap, threadbare in places, and her swollen feet had burst through the sides of her low-heeled shoes. 'I'm Kathleen.' She lifted the tiny bundle in her arms. 'This is Tom.'

'I'm Judith Meredith,' she said and stopped. She didn't know whether she should shake hands or not.

'I know,' Kathleen said shortly. She smiled at the young woman's surprised expression. 'There's not much goes on in the camp that everyone doesn't get to hear about.' She jerked her head towards the van. 'When Mickser brought in the van, he told us that he'd left Spider at the side of the road with a woman. We were all curious about this woman,' she added in a tone which indicated that she was disappointed with what she had seen.

Judith felt a sudden snap of anger at the woman's implication. She opened her mouth to reply, but stopped when Spider appeared, wiping his hands on a filthy rag. He had taken off his leather jacket and his white t-shirt was streaked with oil. He came up behind Kathleen, draped an arm around her shoulder and peered in at the baby.

'Don't you be putting your mucky fingers near the child,' Kathleen snapped.

Judith was surprised—shocked—to find that she felt a twinge of jealousy at the easy familiarity between the two. She wondered if Kathleen was Spider's wife. He looked so young—too young—to be married, but she had the vague idea that travelling people married very young.

'How is the van?' she asked quietly.

Spider made a face. 'Mickser says he might be able to sort it out today, if he can find the part, or maybe early in the morning. If he can, I'll have you in Galway by early afternoon tomorrow.'

Kathleen said something to Spider, the words coming so quickly that Judith missed what she was saying. His expression changed and he shook his head once, 'No.' The woman scowled at him, snapped something that might have been a curse, and marched away. Spider stood looking after her for a moment and shook his head again. Visibly forcing a smile to his lips, he turned back to Judith. 'Come on, let's go for a walk. There's nothing we can do here for the moment.'

Judith nodded gratefully. She felt incredibly uncomfortable in the encampment. It was a different world, and she was no part of it; that was obvious in the way the people looked at her—especially the younger people. She could see the envy and the anger in their eyes. The older people regarded her with quiet acceptance. They had no desire to be like her, to be part of her world.

Spider stopped by the van and lifted a small blue sports bag out from behind the front seat. Throwing his leather jacket over his shoulder, he nudged Mickser, who was still under the van, with his foot. 'I'll be back soon.'

'Take your time, there's nothing you can do here. You'll only be in my way.'

'See you later then.' Spider strode away, the bag swinging to and fro, his scuffed and down-at-heel cowboy boots kicking at the bare, worn earth. Judith had to run to catch up with him. As they neared the entrance to the camp, someone shouted at him, but Spider ignored them, deliberately looking away. Beyond the camp, he slowed his pace and allowed Judith to catch up with him. He glanced sidelong at her and smiled an apology, and then nodded to a narrow opening in the hedge. He squeezed through and then used his bag to keep the thorns and brambles away from her clothes as she followed. They crossed an overgrown field in silence, and followed it over to a steep bank which led down to a swiftly running stream. Spider crouched down by the water's edge and peered into its depths. He pulled his bag up beside him and took out a small glass tumbler and dipped it into the water. Judith thought he was going to drink it, but instead, he held it up to the light and waited until it had settled. Finally satisfied, he poured the water away and then, much to Judith's astonishment, pulled off his dirty t-shirt. From his bag he took out a small cake of soap and proceeded to wash himself in the icy water, hissing with the chill.

'Are you annoyed about something?' Judith asked, aware that the silence was lengthening. 'Have I done something to upset you?'

Spider turned to look at her, his deep-set black eyes wide in astonishment. Pale soapy suds ran down his tanned muscular body. 'You? What could you have done to upset me?'

Judith sat down on the top of the bank, her back against a twisted chestnut tree. She shrugged. 'I don't know. I just got the impression that something happened at the camp to annoy you . . . and that it was something to do with me.'

'Aye . . . well.' He turned away and scrubbed at his oily hands, dirty grey suds staining the water. 'You don't want to mind that. A lot of travelling people aren't too happy around outsiders. Outsiders judge them, try to change them, see only what they want to see.'

'I'm not like that . . .' Judith began.

'You are,' he grinned. 'You don't think so. But you are: it shows in the way you move in the camp, the way you hold yourself, the way you look at people, the way you speak to them. And you're not even aware of it.' He straightened and began to dry himself with a ragged towel. 'I'm not blaming you,' he said quickly. 'The travellers back there act in exactly the same way towards you. And they don't know it either. But I've lived in both worlds, amongst the settled community and the travellers, I know what I'm talking about.'

'What happened back in the camp?' she asked, watching the way the muscles in his shoulders moved beneath his skin as he pulled on another t-shirt. He dipped his dirty t-shirt in the stream and began scrubbing at the stains with the same cake of soap he'd used for washing. 'The old lady said I'd bring you trouble, didn't she? And the young woman, Kathleen, she certainly didn't like me.'

'Ah, well now you don't want to listen to Kathleen. She was just a bit jealous seeing me arrive in the camp with a pretty young woman.' He grinned mischievously. 'She's been trying to get her hands on me for years. She obviously thought that you and me were . . . friends, and that someone had beaten her to it.'

'I thought she looked a little young to have a baby,' Judith remarked.

'Sure, she'd be seventeen, old enough to have a child. But she's not married yet,' he added as if that explained everything. 'The baby's her sister's. She had just come back from the town where she'd been begging. Travelling girls sometimes borrow babies when they're begging: people are inclined to give when they see children.'

'And what about the old woman? She didn't like me either.'

Spider paused, considering. 'No, it wasn't that she didn't like you, she just said that you could bring trouble . . . which is perfectly true.'

Judith knew he was being evasive, but there was no way she could turn the subject back around again. 'I was thinking of heading on,' she said, watching him scrub at the t-shirt.

He looked up in surprise. 'What do you mean, "heading on?"'

'Heading on to Galway.'

'How?'

She shrugged. 'I suppose I could try hitching.'

Spider snorted rudely. 'A young girl hitching alone. You must be out of your mind! There are some crazy people out on the roads.'

'I know, I met one,' she said with a grin.

Spider straightened up and spread his t-shirt on a bush to dry. He scrambled up the bank and sat down beside Judith, swinging his legs out over the edge. He smelt of wood smoke and soap. 'Seriously though,' he said, 'if you go hitchhiking across the country, you stand a very good chance of being picked up by a crazy person . . . or the police.'

She glanced at him sharply. 'The police?'

'Someone is sure to have noticed that you've gone missing by now. The police will have been informed; they'll be on the look-out for a single girl travelling alone. In fact,' he added, 'they always pay special attention to young people—especially young girls—travelling alone.'

'I'm sure I'd be all right,' she mumbled.

'I'd prefer if you didn't,' he said quietly.

'Why?' she asked, surprised.

He shrugged, obviously uncomfortable with the line of questioning. 'I wouldn't like to see anything happen to you,' he said eventually. He glanced sidelong at her quickly, and then turned away. 'If the van is fixed tonight, we'll set out immediately. How's that?'

'It's putting you to a lot of trouble.'

'If I didn't want to do it, I wouldn't,' he said simply.

'But why do you want to do it?' she asked, watching him out of the corner of her eye.

'Because I do. Because . . . because . . . I like you. You're not like any other girl I know. And, maybe it's because you don't seem to have a problem with me being a traveller.'

'I've no problem with you being a traveller,' she said truthfully. 'But Granny Hayes said I'd bring you trouble,' she reminded him. 'I don't want to repay your kindness by landing you in trouble.'

Spider threw back his head and laughed. 'That's nothing new. I've been in trouble all my life.'

'What sort of trouble?' she asked, smiling in return.

'Trouble at school, trouble with my parents, trouble with the police.' He saw her surprised expression and shrugged. 'I was a wild kid.' He laced his fingers behind his head and lay back on the bank, staring up at the cloudless summer sky. 'I kept running away from home as a child, that's when the trouble really started.'

'Why did you run away?'

Spider raised himself up on his elbows. 'Because I was bored.' He grinned, suddenly looking years younger. 'I wanted adventure, excitement. My parents had been travellers and I loved the stories they told about living on the road, about the people they met, the places they visited. It sounded like a great adventure. So I ran away to have an adventure of my own.'

'And was it the great adventure?' she asked quietly. She turned on her side, leaning on her left arm, and looked down at his deeply tanned face. His eyes were closed, and his lips were twisted in something resembling a smile.

Spider opened his left eye and squinted up at her. 'No, it wasn't. I wasn't a traveller. I was simply another runaway kid living rough on the streets of Dublin.' He closed his eye and his mouth drew into a thin hard line. 'I ran away three times before I finally got sense. The first time was great—it was fun and exciting. The second time was different, sometimes I think it was even more exciting, because I knew the ropes by then. The third and last time, I suddenly realised that if I was going to continue doing this, I wasn't going to live very much longer.'

'What was it like living on the streets?'

'Hungry. You were always hungry. And lonely,' he added softly. 'And I don't mean you were alone . . . that was different. Even though you were in the middle of a large city, you knew no-one cared, no-one gave a damn about you.'

'How did you survive?' Judith whispered, trying to imagine what it was like for a child, alone and hungry, wandering around the city.

'I begged. There's no shame in begging. I was quite good at it,' he added, almost proudly. 'If the weather was fine, you could usually get the price of a good meal by the evening.'

'And if you didn't?'

'Then you bought yourself a bar of chocolate or a pack of crisps and made do with that.'

'It sounds awful,' Judith murmured.

'No, not really. I enjoyed myself most of the time. You don't remember the times you were cold and wet, or when you couldn't find a place to sleep for the night, or when the bigger kids picked a fight with you.'

'But why did you do it?' she asked again. 'You must have had a reason other than boredom.'

Spider shrugged. 'I did it because I wanted to. I did it because I could.' He turned his head and, shading his eyes with his hand, looked up at her. 'Have you never done something simply because you wanted to?'

Judith started to shake her head, and then she stopped. 'Just once,' she whispered. 'Like you, I ran away.'

Spider reached over and squeezed her hand. 'Fellow travellers.'

7

Maxwell Meredith stared out across the glittering
expanse of Killiney Bay, the sinking sun throwing
long shadows from the land across the water. Far, far below
a boat, its white sails folded across its decks, rocked at
anchor. He could just about make out the tiny shapes of
figures on the deck; they looked like they were picnicking.

Maxwell turned back to the long, bright room. His
dinner lay uneaten on the glass-topped table, although he
had drunk most of a bottle of expensive Italian wine. An
ornate antique clock on the mantelpiece chimed the hour:
eight o'clock. This time yesterday, the wedding dinner was
just about over and the speeches were about to begin. For
the first time since his wife had died, he had felt whole
again. He had been happy.

Until Judith had disappeared.

His daughter had been missing less than twenty-four
hours, but he felt as if she'd been gone for a lifetime.

Where was she? Where had she gone?

If she had been kidnapped, why hadn't the kidnappers contacted him about a ransom? And if she had run away, where
had she run to? He had spent the entire day phoning everyone
he could possibly think of to whom she might have gone.

His thoughts were running around in circles. Had she been kidnapped, had she run away? But if she'd been kidnapped, then her kidnappers would have contacted him, that stood to reason. All they'd be interested in was money; they wouldn't want to hold onto her any longer than was necessary. So the only conclusion he could arrive at was that she had run away.

But that still didn't answer the question—why had she run away? She had everything a girl could want. Indeed, anything she asked for, she got: the latest fashions, the newest releases, books, videos, toys, the racing bike she simply had to have, but never used, the computer she needed, which she only played games on, the electronic organ she so desperately wanted, but never played. She went to the best schools, went abroad for both her Christmas and summer holidays. Why? Why would she want to run away?

The door opened and Frankie came into the room. She was carrying a wicker tray, balancing a small teapot, milk and sugar, and two matching cups.

Maxwell looked at his wife and attempted to smile. He wanted to say something to her, to apologise for ruining her wedding, the honeymoon, but instead, all he could say was, 'Why? Why did she do it, Frankie?'

'I don't know, Max. Maybe because she was hurt, maybe because she felt angry, betrayed.'

'Betrayed . . . how?' he asked, surprised.

Frankie put the tray down on a side-table by the window and carefully poured the tea. Without looking at her husband, she said quietly, 'Because you married me.' She glanced up when he said nothing. 'You brought another woman into your life, into her life too. And that woman just happened to be her mother's best friend. She's fifteen years old, Maxwell. She's confused. She's no longer a girl, but not quite a woman. We know she hasn't had a boy-friend, she doesn't know many boys, even her brother is fifteen years older than her. Up until now, you've been the only man in her life, and for the last two years she likes to think that she's looked after you. It's not so uncommon for a girl to fixate on her father; boys tend to focus on their mothers.' Frankie added milk and sugar and carried the tea across to Maxwell. He took it from her hands but didn't look at her. His gaze was fixed out across the bay. In the fading light the couple's reflections were clearly visible on the glass, making it look as if they were standing in mid-air over the water. Frankie wrapped her arms around her husband and rested the side of her face against his broad back. 'She's confused. She cannot accept that it is possible to love more than one person at any one time. She thinks that by loving me, you have stopped loving Margaret. Maybe she even thinks you've stopped loving her.'

'But that's ridiculous!'

'I know that. But when was the last time you told her you loved her?'

Maxwell opened his mouth to reply, but closed it again without saying anything.

'And did you even sit her down before the wedding and try to explain to her why we were getting married, explain why you wanted to marry me . . . ?'

'Well . . . well, I meant to. But there was so much work to be done before the wedding, and I was away, and . . . ' He stopped shaking his head, feeling the burning at the back of his throat. 'Where is she, Frankie?' he whispered.

'She'll be back,' Frankie murmured, with a confidence she didn't feel. 'All she needs is some time to work things out for herself, to sort out her feelings.'

'But where is she, Frankie, where is she?'

Frankie hugged Maxwell closer. She had no answer to that.

8

The years he had spent on the streets had given him an unerring instinct for trouble. And his experiences on the streets had taught him to respect that instinct.

And there was trouble on the way now. He could feel it coming.

Although Spider had a reputation on the streets and amongst the travellers as a tearaway, a hooligan and a trouble-maker, that reputation wasn't entirely justified. He preferred to walk away from trouble or to avoid a situation where a confrontation might occur. But when provoked he could be a nasty and vicious fighter, who used every dirty trick to make sure he wasn't the one to get hurt. As the years went by, his reputation alone ensured that people avoided picking an argument with him . . . and that suited him perfectly.

He sat in the open door of his broken-down van, whittling away at a stick of wood with a tiny battered pen-knife. The radio was turned down low, the vague murmur of music sounding as if it was coming from a long distance away. Dusk was falling and the camp had taken on a gritty, grainy air, like a badly focused photograph. Lights had appeared in most of the caravans, most of them run off car batteries, but some were oil lanterns and he could see candles burning in one of the smaller, poorer caravans. The bonfire that had been burning most of the day in the centre of the camp had burnt low and tiny blue flames danced across the ash-whitened logs. Occasionally sparks spiralled heavenwards, and the young man's hard dark eyes turned to follow them until they guttered out.

There was trouble coming.

He turned to look across at Granny Hayes' caravan where Judith was spending the night. A light was burning in the window and he could see the shadows of the two women thrown onto the drawn blinds. They seemed to be laughing.

There was trouble coming, and it was all because of the girl, Judith Meredith.

She was a strange girl. Sometimes he thought she was more child than adult, and yet occasionally she spoke with all the mature authority of an adult . . . or maybe that was just what a good education and money did for you: it made you used to command.

She was pretty; he had to admit that. Tall, blonde, brown-eyed, bright where he was dark, soft where he was hard. She was incredibly ignorant about so many things—she knew absolutely nothing about the travellers, for example—and yet she could obviously read and write and she spoke so well.

Judith Meredith was totally unlike any other girl he had ever met . . . and she seemed to be interested in him. She was certainly interested in listening to him.

Spider continued whittling the stick, stopping only when he had worn it down to a nub. One of the things he enjoyed about travelling was meeting people, strange, curious, interesting, sometimes frightening people. When he had first run away from home he had been constantly frightened by the people he met on the street. It was only later that he realised that they could teach him something, that he could learn from them, learn how to fend for himself, how to survive. He turned to look at the lighted caravan window again, and wondered what he could learn from Judith Meredith.

The caravan was small, incredibly cluttered and smelt stale and airless. But the old woman had offered her a bed for the night and she could hardly refuse, since the alternative was to sleep in the van. Once she got over her initial fear of the old woman, she found her a rather lovely person, gentle, kind and considerate. Just like a granny in fact.

The van had stubbornly refused to be fixed. In the late afternoon, Judith had watched Spider slide out from beneath it and hop into the driver's seat. For a single heartbeat the engine came to life only to die again almost immediately afterwards, thick black smoke billowing from the exhaust. As he strolled past her, wiping his hands on an oily rag, he muttered, 'Remind me to get another van.' She saw him head out of the camp, heading down the road, and she knew he was going to the stream to wash in the icy water.

'You'll not be going anywhere tonight, love.' Granny Hayes had come up behind Judith and was staring after Spider.

Judith turned to the old woman. 'No, no, I suppose not.' She looked away quickly. She found the woman's bright green eyes unsettling. 'Maybe tomorrow,' she murmured.

The old woman nodded. 'Aye. But you're welcome to stay the night with me. I've a spare bed and no-one will bother you.' Judith looked at her in alarm, but Granny Hayes smiled and patted her hand. 'I didn't put that very well, did I? What I meant, dear, was that you wouldn't be disturbed tonight.' She grinned as she saw Judith look across the camp to where Spider's van sat. 'It wouldn't be right for you to sleep in the van—especially as that's where Spider will be sleeping.'

'But I slept there last night . . .' Judith began and then stopped, suddenly realising what the old woman was leading up to. She felt colour burn on her cheeks.

Granny Hayes patted her hand. 'Don't worry, my dear. I wasn't suggesting anything. I know Spider too well. But amongst the travellers, unmarried men and women do not sleep together.'

'Have I caused problems for Spider?'

Granny Hayes didn't immediately reply. Instead she linked her arm through Judith's and led her across the camp. The old woman's head barely came to the girl's shoulder. 'What do you want me to say to you?' she mused aloud.

'The truth,' Judith said quietly.

Granny Hayes nodded. 'I've always believed in the truth, so I'll give you that. But often the truth isn't pleasant. People find it easier to lie, because the lie doesn't hurt . . . but in the long run, if the lie is discovered for what it was, then it hurts. I suppose that's the long way of telling you that yes, you have caused him problems. And I did tell him that you would bring trouble down on him . . . and this was not done to hurt you, I was just stating a fact.' She squeezed Judith's arm to take the sting out from her words. 'You're obviously a very nice girl. And you have your problems, I can sense that in you. I would have liked to ask you not to share your problems with Spider, but it's too late for that, much too late. Now, while he has become part of your problem, you have become his problem.' She led the way up the steps to her small caravan and pushed open the door. She slid a kettle onto a gas ring and, without turning around, she said, 'Sometimes it helps to talk . . .'

The first of the men returned to the camp around midnight. They had been in the local pub since the early evening and they were very drunk. Weaving to and fro, they wound their way through the caravans, singing loudly, their broad accents making the words of the song sound foreign and exotic. A dog started barking.

Close to twelve-thirty there was another influx into the camp as the remainder of the men and women who had gone drinking returned. Most were on foot, but a couple of vans pulled into the camp, engines screaming, radios thumping, horns blaring. Car doors slammed, and there was more shouting and singing. In the caravan beside Granny Hayes' a baby started crying.

Judith had been dozing just as the first people had returned to the camp. She had lain in the tiny bed, her heart thumping with fright as the voices appeared to approach the caravan she was in. But they died away one by one as people made their way to their own caravans and for a while there was silence.

Judith lay in the narrow cot bed, listening to the gentle night-time noises of the camp. She was lying directly beneath a window and she could see out into the cloudless sky. The stars were hard and sharp and brilliant over her head. For the first time since the wedding she wondered what her father was doing. Her father and step-mother. Had they gone away on their honeymoon and come back, or had they been forced to cancel it altogether?

Judith wrapped her arms tightly around herself, blinking hard as the stars shifted and swam in sudden tears. She hadn't wanted to do that to them. But she hadn't thought about that. That was her problem: she didn't think, she acted. Even in school, she had the habit of opening her mouth and putting her foot in it.

She had had a long talk with Granny Hayes. The old woman hadn't really been curious about Judith, she hadn't asked any questions, and yet Judith found herself telling her the whole story. Even as she was speaking, she had begun to understand what it must sound like to this woman who had lived most of her life on the side of the road in a caravan: a spoilt bitch talking about running away from her half-a-million pound house in Killiney. Her school fees alone must cost more than the woman saw in a year. She suddenly discovered that she was embarrassed. But Granny Hayes had merely listened, shaking her head every now and again, nodding in the correct places. When she had finished, having told the story right up to the point where Spider had brought her into the camp, Judith finally managed to ask her what she had meant about Spider becoming part of her problem, and she becoming Spider's problem.

'Think about it, girl,' the old woman had murmured, her green eyes bright over the rim of a teacup. 'You ran away and found yourself in trouble. Spider saved you. He could have walked away, but he took it on himself to take you to Galway. He became involved with you because of your problem.' She put the cup down and looked into Judith's eyes. 'But, my dear, he wouldn't have gotten into that fight if you hadn't been there; he wouldn't have had to go to Galway if he hadn't met up with you. His van wouldn't have broken down if he'd had a chance to fix it in Dublin. He wouldn't have had to bring you here and there wouldn't be all this fuss about it.' She smiled again and spread her hands. 'You are his problem.'

Judith glanced out through the curtained window. Squinting shortsightedly, she could just about make out Spider sitting in the open door of his van. He was doing something with his hands, but she couldn't see what.

'Have I got him into trouble?' she asked quietly. 'I didn't mean to.'

'No, not trouble exactly. Not real trouble. But girl, if you stay very much longer with Spider, I can see trouble ahead for both of you. And these aren't the wise words of a Gypsy wisewoman, or some such nonsense, this is just common sense speaking. You're from two different worlds; you're like oil and water. You don't mix.' She poured more tea for Judith. 'You've caused a bit of a stir by arriving here with him. A lot of the girls have their eye on Spider. He'll make a good match,' she added, watching Judith closely. 'He's kind, gentle and hardworking. You've already discovered that he'll go out of his way to do you a favour, but when he's pushed, he stands his ground. I don't think you can ask much more of a man, do you?'

Judith looked out of the window again and shook her head slightly. She had never really thought about it before, but she supposed Granny Hayes was right. What did you look for in a man, a boyfriend, a husband?

'Oh, and he's handsome too,' Granny Hayes added with a cheeky grin, 'but I think you've already noticed that.'

Judith was abruptly glad that the interior of the caravan was dark as she felt her cheeks burn a bright warm red.

Now she lay in the narrow cot thinking back on what the old woman had said. Just what did girls look for in a man? What had Frankie looked for in her father? He was everything Granny Hayes said Spider was, he was kind, gentle and hardworking, and she also knew that he was a ruthless businessman. He was handsome too . . . and wealthy, very, very wealthy. When Judith had first heard that Frankie was going to marry her father, she had immediately assumed it was for his enormous wealth . . . but Frankie was the heir to a huge fortune of her own, so it couldn't be the money. She was suddenly forced to consider the possibility that Frankie might actually love her father. It was something she had never thought about before: she hadn't even allowed herself to think about it.

Kathleen stood in the shadows and watched Granny Hayes' caravan. She was swaying slightly from side to side. She wasn't drunk exactly, just . . . relaxed. She hadn't drunk more than three halves, or maybe it had been four, but she'd eaten nothing all day except a couple of bars of chocolate and the drink had gone straight to her head.

She'd been thinking about the city girl all day, ever since she had watched her walk in alongside Spider, all cosy and friendly like. Just who did she think she was? Oh, she'd heard the story they'd told about her being attacked by three gurriers and Spider coming to the rescue. Well that was just so much rubbish. Did they think she was a fool? For a start, what was a girl like that doing in a situation where she was going to be attacked by three thugs? She was educated, and she certainly didn't look stupid. No, it was all a lie. The only part of their story that was true was the bit about Spider's van breaking down. Why hadn't they come in with Mickser in the truck? Maybe they just wanted a cosy little walk together. And this afternoon, when they'd left the site, where had they gone? Well, she'd watched them across the field. she'd seen them head down towards the stream, and then she'd seen Spider pull off his t-shirt.

So what did a girl like that want with Spider? Maybe she liked slumming it. What did she do, bring him to her fancy parties and show him off to her fancy friends? And what did she call him: was he a traveller, a gypsy, or an itinerant, or a tinker, or a knacker, or . . .

Well, Spider was hers. Oh, nothing had ever been said, but she had known Spider since they were small children together. She even knew his real name. They had always got on very well together, and whenever they met on the road, he'd always make a point of having a drink with her. She'd seen the way he looked at her with his large black eyes . . . and this afternoon, he'd looked at the city girl the same way.

Well, she wasn't going to have him.

Maybe in the city they had no regard for another girl's man, but the little bitch was about to find out that the travelling people looked after their own.

Taking a deep breath, Kathleen stepped out of the shadows and strode towards Granny Hayes' caravan.

Judith awoke with her heart beating time to the pounding on the caravan door. She sat up in the bed, pulling the thin blanket up to her chin. She could hear a young woman's voice raised in a high-pitched, unintelligible scream.

There was the rasp of a match and a light flared. Granny Hayes appeared, her features turned into a mask by the wavering candlelight.

'What is it?' Judith hissed.

'Nothing to be worried about. Some drunk knocking on the wrong caravan. Go back to sleep, I'll take care of it.' She moved down to the other end of the caravan and opened the door. 'Go home, you're drunk,' she snapped. 'You should be ashamed of yourself.'

The woman outside said something quickly, but Judith only caught the last few words. '. . . speak to her.'

'No,' Granny Hayes said firmly.

'Let me speak to her!' The voice was louder now, almost screaming.

Judith crept from her bed and peered out through the curtains. Lights were appearing in the caravans and someone turned on car headlights, bathing the front of Granny Hayes' caravan in stark white light. Squinting against the glare, Judith recognised Kathleen, the young woman with the baby who had spoken to her earlier that day.

'Go home. Sleep it off.' Granny Hayes' voice was ice cold and angry.

'No. I want her out of here. I want her away from my man.'

Judith abruptly realised that the young woman was talking about her. But what man was she talking about? The realisation that it could only be Spider dawned just as he appeared out of the crowd. His face was set into a hard mask, his mouth a thin straight line. His left hand locked around Kathleen's upper arm, his fingers biting into her flesh as he spun her about. He bent his head close to hers and spoke quickly and quietly. Judith didn't hear what he said, but she judged by his expression that he was angry.

Kathleen spat back at him and attempted to pull her arm free, but it was locked in a vice-like grip. She drew back her left hand and swung at him, but Spider caught her hand and forced it down. 'Enough!' he snapped.

'Stop this, both of you,' Granny Hayes shouted.

Two young men suddenly pushed through the crowd. They were both red-haired and bore a startling resemblance to Kathleen. The smaller of them had a short stick in his hand.

'SPIDER!' Judith screamed, hammering on the window.

Spider looked up as the taller of the two brothers leapt at him. Pushing Kathleen away, sending her sprawling in the dirt, he jumped forward into the young man, hitting with his shoulder squarely in the centre of his chest. Kathleen's brother staggered backwards and sat down hard on the ground, gasping for breath. The younger brother moved in quickly, swinging the stick from side to side. His face was twisted into a feral grin.

Judith saw Spider's hands close into tight fists. Turning sideways, he suddenly leaned back, and snapped out with his right foot. The metal tip on his cowboy boot struck the younger man in the wrist, sending the stick spinning off into the shadows. The youth staggered away, clutching his wrist, white-faced with pain. Spider turned to look at the silent crowd. 'Anyone else?' he demanded.

Granny Hayes suddenly appeared at Judith's side. 'I think you'd better get ready to go,' she said urgently. There was no malice in her voice as she continued. 'Don't come back here, you're not welcome. And if you want to repay Spider for all he's done for you, leave him as quickly as possible. Return to your world as soon as you can; allow him to return to his.'

Judith turned to look out the window to where the crowd was slowly dispersing, only Kathleen and her two brothers remaining.

Granny Hayes lifted the curtain and looked at the silent trio. 'They've lost face in front of their family and friends. They're not going to forgive you or Spider for that.'

Spider waited until Kathleen had turned her back and stalked away, followed, a few moments later, by her brothers, before he finally came into the caravan. He was shaking his head slightly, opening and closing his fists, as he fought to control his temper. Granny Hayes came over and took his arms, looking up into his dark eyes. 'You did what you had to do,' she said firmly.

Spider nodded. He looked past Granny Hayes and found Judith's eyes. 'We have to go,' he sighed. He jerked his head. 'I'm sorry you had to see that.'

'I'm sorry I caused it.'

Spider kissed Granny Hayes on the cheek. 'I'll come back in a while,' he murmured, 'maybe next year, maybe the year after.'

And Judith suddenly realised what she had cost the young traveller.

Monday 30th July

9

HEIRESS MISSING

Police are investigating the disappearance of Judith Meredith, daughter of wealthy industrialist, Maxwell Meredith.

Miss Meredith, (15), was last seen two days ago, when she was a bridesmaid at her father's wedding to popular socialite, Frances Rourke-Heffernan. Judith Meredith is blonde, brown-eyed, five foot one inch tall, and is described as looking older than fifteen.

Sources close to the Meredith family confirmed that Maxwell Meredith and his bride have cancelled their honeymoon in Hawaii and are now anxiously awaiting developments. There are unconfirmed reports that a substantial reward is about to be offered for information leading to her safe return.

A police spokesman said that they are treating the girl's disappearance as 'suspicious' but that it was too early to begin speculating about a possible kidnapping.

10

Judith dozed on and off for the remainder of the night. Her dreams were troubled, but when she awoke she had no conscious memory of them, except that she had been running, running, running, looking for something, something that was always just out of sight.

She awoke in the chill pre-dawn and sat up in the narrow bed to look out the window. The light from a high-intensity torch seared into the darkness and she found Spider working beneath the van. She wondered if he had been there all night.

Judith got up as the first glimmer of dawn was breaking across the sky and splashed ice-cold water onto her face. It took her a few minutes to figure out how to use the gas ring, but she finally managed to boil a kettle and make some tea. There was no sound from Granny Hayes' curtained-off cubicle, so she poured two mugs, added milk and sugar to both—she remembered Spider took three spoons of sugar—cracked open the caravan door and carried them out into the chill morning air. Her breath smoked before her face and she shivered, scalding tea splashing onto her hands. The ground underfoot was soft and she felt herself sinking slightly as she made her way through the puddles.

Spider slid out from beneath the van when he saw the boots approach. He was wearing a pair of ancient green overalls and a black wool cap. His hands were filthy and his face was smeared with oil and grease. He grinned at Judith as he gratefully accepted the tea.

'Aaah, thanks luv, just what I needed.' He crouched down with his back to the tyre and breathed deeply. He looked tired, and there were deep dark circles beneath his eyes. Judith squatted beside him, her hands wrapped around the teacup for warmth.

'I'm sorry,' she began.

'Don't be,' he said quickly.

'But I've caused you nothing but trouble . . .'

'Trouble comes to all of us,' he grinned. 'If you're due your share of misfortune, it will get you one way or the other.'

'That's an extraordinary attitude.'

'Not really. Sooner or later everyone realises that there are things you can change, things you have control over, and other things, other circumstances outside your control. All you can do then is accept them. Roll with the punches.'

'And I'm a punch?' she smiled.

'A knockout.'

The van started up with a roar and a stuttering backfire that must have woken up the entire camp. A cloud of thick acrid smoke fouled the fresh morning air.

Spider grinned at Judith as he carefully eased the van into gear. 'I don't know how far this will get us, but so long as it gets us away from here we're all right.'

The van lurched away across the soft ground, the engine growling, a rattling knock deep in its heart. The gears crunched as Spider wrestled the steering wheel.

'What's wrong?' Judith asked, feeling the vibration deep in her bones.

'What's right,' Spider grinned. 'I practically built this myself from bits and pieces of other vans. I'm surprised it goes at all. The engine is just about finished, we've blown a cylinder head gasket, we need new plugs, new filters and probably a new radiator.'

The van lurched, its wheels spinning as they came up out of the soft earth onto the hard tarmacked road.

'Will we make Galway today?' Judith wondered.

Spider smiled tightly. 'Don't count on it. I don't think we'll even reach the next town.'

'You could have stayed,' Judith said, watching him closely.

'Not really. It was about time I moved on anyway.'

'That girl, Kathleen, is she your girlfriend?'

'I don't have any girlfriends,' he said shortly.

'Why not?'

He shrugged. 'I've no time.' He glanced sidelong at her. 'And what about you—have you any boyfriends?'

Judith shook her head.

'None?' Spider asked, astonished, 'I would have thought that a pretty girl like you would have loads of admirers.'

'Like you, I've no time,' she smiled.

Spider grinned. He pressed the accelerator and the knocking in the engine turned into a steady whine and rattle. He eased off the accelerator and the noise died away to a more acceptable level. He looked at the speedometer and shook his head. 'At twenty-two miles an hour, we're never going to reach Galway.'

'Is there anything we can do?' Judith inquired.

'We can ditch the van and continue on foot or we can try hitching. I'm supposed to be meeting my uncle in Galway. I'll borrow some money from him and come back and have the van seen to.'

'I could get you some money in Galway . . .' Judith began, but Spider shook his head emphatically. 'Don't worry about it.'

They drove on in silence for a while, and then Judith asked, 'What did Kathleen want last night? What did she mean that you were her man?'

'Who knows?' he said lightly.

'You do,' she stated flatly.

Spider nodded slowly. 'I've told you, she was jealous. Ignore her. Forget it ever happened. She'd had a few drinks and she wanted to fight you.'

'Fight me!'

'And that's not a fight you'd have won,' he added with a grin. 'I've seen her fight before.' He saw the look on Judith's face and continued, 'Don't look so shocked.'

She shrugged. 'I'm not shocked. I'm just surprised. When a guy goes off with another girl, the girls don't fight where . . .'

'. . . where you come from,' he finished. 'So what do they do? They talk about one another, bitch about it, and do one another down to their friends. But you know something,' he added, 'I bet they'd really like to fight.'

Judith thought about it for a moment, and then she grinned. 'You know, I think you're right.'

They drove in companionable silence for the best part of an hour, until Spider suddenly swore and stood hard on the brakes, pulling the van into the side of the road. White steam was billowing up in front of the windscreen. He pounded on the steering wheel in frustration, and then his shoulders slumped. 'End of the road,' he muttered.

'Can you fix it?'

'Yes . . . no . . . maybe. I'm sure I can patch it up, but it'll take time.' He sat forward and squinted down the length of the road. 'We're about a mile outside of Kinnegad. Why don't you go on into the town and get us some food and something to drink. Maybe by the time you get back, I'll have sorted out this mess.' He dug into his jacket pocket and pulled out a crumpled five pound note.

Judith ignored it. 'I've got some money of my own. What do you want?'

'Anything,' he muttered. 'Whatever you like yourself.' He shoved open his door and climbed out into the cool morning air.

Judith climbed out her side and came around the front of the van, but Spider was already flat on his back on the road beneath it. She could hear a steady stream of muttered curses. Smiling to herself, she turned and set off down the road. He wasn't like any boy she had ever met before. Although she had never had a regular boyfriend, she knew dozens of boys, most of whom were brothers or cousins of her friends. She found they compared rather unfavourably with Spider; comparing them to him was rather like comparing a mature man to a boy. He seemed so sure of himself, so calm, so confident. And yet in some ways he was just a boy. He was only a couple of years older than herself. But Granny Hayes was right: they were from different worlds. There were times though when he seemed so shy, and times when she could sense that he didn't know how to act around her. Like now, for example. When he had climbed out of the van, he had started to work on it immediately. He hadn't waited to see if she would agree to go into the town and buy some food, he had just assumed that she would. When he had offered her money and she had refused, he hadn't pressed her, simply put his own money back in his pocket.

A sudden thought struck her and she stopped by the side of the road. He had assumed that she'd be back. And what was even more surprising was that she hadn't even considered not coming back to him!

It took her about forty minutes to walk into Kinnegad. Her boots might look stylish, but the narrow high heel was not designed for any serious walking and by the time she reached the town she was hobbling.

Kinnegad was like most Irish towns, a long main street, lined with shops and pubs. There was a turning to the left just as she entered the town, signposting the road to Galway. She stood at the junction for a few moments, watching two blonde-haired girls—they looked German—with knapsacks on their backs standing a couple of yards away from the junction. They were holding a large cardboard sign with

GALWAY printed in strong black letters. Even as she watched, a car pulled in and they climbed inside. Judith remembered what Spider had said about hitching and wondered how dangerous it really was. She crossed the road and stopped to look at herself in the window of a fast-food restaurant. Her blonde hair was uncombed and tangled, already beginning to look greasy—she usually washed it once a day—and she hadn't applied any make-up. She realised she felt gritty, even her teeth felt furred. There were stains on her jacket and the knees of her trousers and her boots and the cuffs of her jeans were splashed with dried brown mud. She dropped her chin down onto her chest . . . and then grimaced with distaste. She was beginning to smell too.

Judith raised her head and smiled ruefully at her reflection. The day before yesterday she had been bridesmaid at the most stylish wedding of the year . . . but now she doubted if any of the guests would recognise her. She looked like a traveller. But she also realised how easy it was to look like a traveller when there was no running water, no showers and no washing machines.

She stopped in the first grocer's she came to and bought a small sliced pan, a quarter pound of butter, some cooked ham, tomatoes, a pint of milk and teabags, two cans of coke and a copy of *The Irish Times*. There was surprisingly little change out of a fiver.

It was only when she came out of the grocer's that she realised she was exhausted. Hardly surprising though—she had only got a couple of hours' sleep the previous night and not much more the night before. She trudged out of the town, dreading the long walk back to the van. She had passed the last building on the road out of Kinnegad when she decided that she had to stop: her feet felt as if they were on fire. The next pair of shoes she bought, she would buy for comfort and never mind fashion. Placing the plastic bag of messages on the ground, she leaned against a low stone wall and thought about pulling off her boots. They felt as if they were cutting into her flesh, but she was afraid that if she took them off and her feet were swollen, she wouldn't be able to get them back on again. Dropping down into a crouch, with her back to the wall, she reached into the bag and pulled out one of the cans of coke. It was still icy cool, and she rubbed the sweating can to her forehead, before pulling back the tab and taking an enormous swallow. She could feel the sugar-laden drink rush through her system, giving her a false energy, and her stomach rumbled, reminding her that she hadn't had breakfast yet.

A car passed her, slowing as it entered the outskirts of the town. She saw the driver—a middle-aged man, fat, balding—looking at her, saw the expression of disgust that flickered across his face.

She had almost finished the can when the second car passed. The driver was a woman and there were two teenagers in the back of the car. The woman glanced at her, and then looked away quickly as if she were embarrassed. The two girls in the back shifted in their seats to stare back at her. They were both smiling. One said something to the other and they laughed.

Judith Meredith picked up the plastic bag and straightened. She popped the empty can into a litter bin and, taking a deep breath, set off down the road, heading back to Spider.

The expressions of the two drivers, male and female—disgust and embarrassment—stayed with her on the long road out of the town.

Did it take so little, she wondered—a dirty face, unwashed hair, grubby clothes—to change our perception of people?

11

Despite what he had said to Judith, Spider had serious doubts about his ability to get the van mobile again. It needed a new engine, a new exhaust, new everything, and while he was an expert at scrounging bits and pieces, getting a whole new engine was beyond even him. All he could do now was to get the van mobile and sell it at the best possible price. He'd give it a good cleaning, spruce it up and he knew a couple of tricks that would make the engine sound as good as new . . . for maybe twenty miles. After that the exhaust might fall off and the engine fall out—but he planned to be long gone by that time.

And speaking of long gone . . . he wondered where Judith had got to. She'd been gone for over an hour.

In the shadows beneath the van Spider smiled at his own reaction. He was actually worried about her. He had to admit that she'd made quite an impression on him; she was unlike any of the female travellers he knew. They were hard, strong women, sure of themselves, confident, able to take care of themselves . . . they had to be. But Judith was none of these things; perhaps it was her vulnerability that drew him to her. She needed him . . . and it had been a long time since anyone had needed him.

Tyres crunched on gravel and he turned his head in time to see what looked like a van pull in behind him. Probably someone offering to help . . . well, he wasn't proud enough to refuse any offer of help. The van doors opened and two people hopped out. He saw jeans and battered cowboy boots and jeans and brand new trainers approaching.

He had started to slide out from beneath the van when the pain swept up through his groin in a solid mass. He spasmed in agony and jerked upright, smashing his head against the under-side of the van. The back of his head struck against the road as it fell back. Red and black lights darted before his eyes, and there was the bloody taste of copper in his mouth where he had bitten into his tongue. He tried to scramble under the van, but someone had grabbed hold of both legs and was roughly hauling him out, while someone else rained kicks and blows down on him, catching him in the stomach, chest and back.

Sick and dazed, he found himself looking up into the leering faces of Kathleen and her two brothers.

'Hello, Spider,' Kathleen whispered, 'we've some unfinished business. Where's your girl friend? I want to have a talk with her.'

'You're too late,' Spider mumbled, blood on his lips, staining his teeth. 'When the van broke down she left.'

'Maybe she'll come back,' Kathleen hissed.

'I don't think so,' Spider murmured. I hope not, he prayed.

Judith stopped when she saw the second van parked behind Spider's. It might be nothing . . . but then again. If she'd learned anything from Spider, she had learned caution. She stepped off the road, where she could keep an eye on the van without being seen, and squinted hard at it. Without her glasses, it was difficult to make out details, but as far as she could see, there was no sign of Spider on the ground working beneath the van.

Leaving her plastic bag of groceries on the ground beneath a thorn bush, she began to make her way down towards the van, keeping behind the hedge that ran alongside the road.

When she came abreast of Spider's battered van, she carefully parted the bushes and peered inside. It looked empty and there was no sign of anyone beneath it, but she could hear voices coming from the second van. They were probably friends of Spider's, travellers who'd spotted the broken-down van and stopped for a chat. He'd laugh when she told him what she'd done. She was about to step out from behind the hedge and walk boldly around to the second van when she stopped. She'd come this far; it wouldn't hurt just to take a peek first, would it?

Moving stealthily through the bushes, she carefully parted the twisted branches. Her heart began beating a rapid tattoo in her chest: Kathleen and her two brothers were crouched behind the van, smoking. The two brothers were sitting on the rear bumper, while Kathleen squatted in front of them, occasionally leaning to one side to peer down the road towards Kinnegad. They were waiting for her.

Her first concern was for Spider. Where was he? He wouldn't have run away—someone like Spider would never run from a fight—which meant that he was either in his own van . . . or theirs. Theirs, she decided. They could keep an eye on him more easily.

All she had to do now was to decide what to do.

Going back into Kinnegad was out of the question: it was too far for a start and it would mean answering too many questions. She could simply walk away. The cold thought curled inside her head like a dark serpent. If she walked away, she reasoned, then Kathleen and her brothers would have no further argument with Spider, and everything would be as it was. But no, everything would not be as it was; it could never again be as it was. She had come into Spider's world, touched it, left her mark on it, just as he had entered her cosy little world and left his own mark there. She couldn't walk away. For lots of reasons.

Lying on her stomach, heedless of her precious denims or outrageously expensive blouse, she crept back to the hedge where she could see the three travellers. She watched them for ten minutes before the plan began forming at the back of her mind. The two brothers didn't move. They simply sat on the bumper, smoking, murmuring quietly amongst themselves. Kathleen though was more nervous: she kept glancing out to the right of the van every few minutes.

It took seven sweating minutes for Judith to manoeuvre her way quietly beneath the hedge. When she came to her feet she was standing up against the passenger door which was tight against the hedgerow. She knew if anyone looked around this side of the van now, she was well and truly caught. Standing on her toes, she peered into the back of the van . . . and discovered Spider! He lay in a crumpled heap on the metal floor, curled into a tight ball, a dark stain on his forehead, bruises on his face. She realised with horror that the stain on his forehead was blood.

Taking deep, deep breaths to calm herself, she looked over at the driver's seat and her heart leapt when she discovered that the keys were in the ignition. Now, if this was truly her lucky day, the passenger door would be unlocked.

It wasn't.

Judith pressed her head against the cool glass for a dozen pounding heartbeats, while she attempted to make a decision. The driver's side was sure to be open, but Kathleen kept looking around that side of the van.

Alternatives?

There weren't any.

Taking a deep breath Judith walked on her toes around the side of the van. She was watching the rear of the van and actually had her hand on the door handle when Kathleen poked her head around and looked straight into her eyes. For a single moment the two young women looked at one another, and then they both shouted together.

Judith wrenched the van door open and flung herself inside, snapping the lock down as Kathleen's wild-eyed vicious face appeared at the window. She was screaming unintelligibly and hammering on the window with her shoe.

Judith turned the key in the ignition. It screeched like a banshee, and then she slammed the van into gear and let off the handbrake just as the sliding door was flung open. Kathleen was caught with one foot in the van and the other still on the road as Judith took off at high speed. She was thrown away from the van and crashed into her elder brother, sending them both rolling into the road.

Gripping the steering wheel tightly, the engine howling in first gear, Judith concentrated on manoeuvring the van through Kinnegad. She nearly missed the left-hand turn for Galway, and took the corner too fast, wheels screaming, bringing shopkeepers to their doors.

She had actually begun to relax and was easing her foot off the accelerator when the hand fell on her shoulder. She almost crashed the van with fright. She looked up into Spider's bloody and battered face.

His hands tightened on both shoulders and then he leaned forward and kissed the top of her head. 'Thanks for coming back.'

'You knew I'd be back,' she said calmly, although her heart was thundering.

He nodded tiredly as he slid into the passenger seat. 'I thought you might.' He waved his hand vaguely at the van. 'But you didn't have to do what you did.'

Judith glanced sidelong at him. 'Oh, but I did,' she whispered. 'I wanted to.'

'You're an extraordinary woman, Judith Meredith,' Spider said quietly.

When she looked at him again, he was asleep.

12

'That was a very brave thing you did,' Spider muttered through clenched teeth as Judith wiped the ugly gash on his forehead with antiseptic.

The young woman grunted, but said nothing. She was concentrating on cleaning the wound where Spider had struck his head on the underside of the van. There was a four inch horizontal wound just above his eyes, which were already beginning to swell. It had bled profusely and Spider's face was a bruised and bloody mask. This was as close as she had ever been to a serious injury, and the last time she had seen this amount of blood was when she had fallen off her bicycle as a child and gashed both knees. She knew that if she was distracted, even for a moment, she was going to throw up.

'I would have loved to have seen the looks on their faces when you took off in their van,' Spider laughed. He remembered watching an old traveller having the palm of his hand sewn up where he had gashed it on a piece of barbed wire. The man was calmly chatting away to Granny Hayes, completely ignoring what she was doing to his flesh with needle and thread. 'Doesn't it hurt?' he had asked the old man. 'Only if I think about it. And while you're talking, you're not thinking,' he replied.

Spider had believed him then, but right now he'd just discovered that either the old man was wrong or that he himself was not doing something right.

'You could have been hurt,' he said through gritted teeth. 'Kathleen was really out to get you.'

'Jealous,' Judith whispered.

'Yea, obviously, but why? I mean we left the camp; what has she to be jealous of now?'

'She saw you with another woman . . .' Judith began, and then stopped. She looked up, a wry smile twisting her lips. When she had first seen her father with Frankie, she had felt exactly as Kathleen had: she had wanted to tear her rival's eyes out. She had been jealous.

'I've seen her fight,' Spider added, 'and you definitely don't want to fight that woman.'

They were parked in a narrow country lane, somewhere beyond Kinnegad. Spider was sitting in the open side door of the Hiace while Judith stood before him—as close as anyone had ever stood to him—so close he could smell the heat from her body.

Judith soaked the hem she had torn from her blouse in some bottled water and wrapped it around Spider's forehead. The centre of the makeshift bandage immediately stained red. The young man hissed in pain.

'It'll do until I can get something better,' Judith said quickly, relieved that she didn't have to look at the wound. She stood back and looked critically at Spider's face. There was a livid bruise on his jaw, his bottom lip was split and there was a long scrape mark down his cheek where it looked as if rigid fingers had dug into his skin. 'Where else are you hurt?' she asked.

'They kicked me in . . . well, they kicked me,' he said, colour coming to his cheeks. 'I think a couple of my ribs may be cracked.'

'We need to get you to hospital,' Judith said, crouching down to look him in the eye.

'No hospital,' Spider said firmly. 'No.'

'But why not? We can go into Casualty, get you patched up and be on our way again.' She nodded at his forehead. 'I think you might need a stitch in that.'

'No hospitals,' Spider repeated. 'My mother went into a hospital with a pain in her stomach: she never came out.'

'But Spider . . .'

'No.'

Judith sighed. 'OK, please yourself, but remember, you'll get no sympathy from me when you start complaining of headaches, or maybe seeing double.'

'Seeing double?' he asked quickly.

'Concussion,' she said dramatically.

'What's concussion?' Spider whispered. 'I don't know the word.'

'It's when . . . it's when you get a violent blow on the head and it sort of shakes things up inside,' she explained as simply as possible. 'You might start seeing two of everything, or hearing noises in your ears, or you might start falling asleep without warning. You might even start forgetting things,' she added earnestly. 'I really wish you'd go to hospital. I'll go with you.'

'They ask too many questions.'

'I'll answer the questions,' Judith said quickly, spotting the break in his defences. She realised he was frightened, and immediately felt ashamed because she had deliberately set out to frighten him. But it was for his own good.

'They might report it to the police. Hospitals do that.'

'Only if it's a wound, like a gunshot wound or a knife wound,' Judith reassured him. She wasn't sure if that was entirely true, but she remembered something her father said about business. 'When you've something to say, say it with absolute confidence, even if you don't believe in it yourself.'

'Please, Spider,' Judith whispered.

'But there'll be forms . . .'

Judith made a face.

'And I can't write,' he said very softly, looking into her wide brown eyes, waiting for a reaction.

'I'll fill in all the forms,' she replied without hesitation.

Spider struggled to come to his feet. Judith reached out and gripped his left arm, helping him up. His right arm was doubled across his body, cradling his sore ribs. He took a deep breath and winced. 'Where's the nearest hospital?' he asked.

You saw all sorts in Casualty, but this pair, Aisling Miller decided, had got to be the strangest. She'd spotted them the moment they came in, and she'd immediately tagged them as travellers. She groaned inwardly, although the smile fixed to her lips never faltered. She'd had a group of travellers in on Saturday night, two men and two women. They were all very drunk. One of the women had fallen and cut herself, and while it was a straightforward bandaging, the four of them had caused absolute chaos in the busy Casualty Department.

'Hello, what's the matter here?' she asked, hurrying up to the couple. The girl—mid to late teens—seemed fine, but the boy—about the same age—was in obvious pain. His face was cut and bruised and there was a crude bandage around his forehead.

'He fell off his motorcycle,' Judith said simply.

It was the voice and the accent that surprised Aisling: it was a cultured, monied upper-class Dublin accent. She was even more surprised when the boy spoke, because his accent was unmistakably a traveller's.

'I've hurt my ribs, bashed my head.'

'Let's have a look at you then.' She waved Spider towards an empty cubicle and looked at Judith. 'If you would like to take a seat in the waiting-room . . . There may be a little delay, I'm afraid,' she added.

'I'll stay with my brother if you don't mind.'

The young nurse wasn't able to hide the expression of

disbelief that flitted across her face. Brother and sister! The pair might be many things . . . but they were certainly not brother and sister. She ushered them into the empty cubicle and helped the young man up onto the plastic-covered table. She made him lean back while she undid the bandage, which had been torn from some silky substance . . . the same material as the girl's blouse, she realised abruptly. Rubbing the material between her fingers, she recognised it as silk—pure silk.

There was something wrong here.

There was an ugly gash on the boy's forehead, but the wound was clean, with no visible dirt in it. The doctor would probably want an X-Ray though. She turned his head from side to side, watching his eyes, looking for signs of concussion. 'That's a nasty scrape; how did it happen?' she asked quietly.

The boy's eyes flickered towards the girl, who was standing behind and to her right. 'I fell off my motorcycle,' he said.

Aisling looked at the wound again; if he'd fallen off a motorbike his flesh should be scraped and torn. She lifted his hands but, except for bruising on the knuckles, the skin was intact. This boy had been in a fight! 'What's your name?'

'Sp . . Simon.'

'Well, Simon, we'll have you fixed up in no time. Now, did you say your ribs hurt?'

He nodded.

Aisling helped him out of his leather jacket. She took the opportunity to turn it over carefully as she laid it on the back of a chair. Again, if he'd come off a bike, the leather jacket should be scraped and torn. Easing off his stained t-shirt, she ran cool fingers along his lower ribs, which were already beginning to purple with bruises. The young man winced and bit his lips as she pressed.

'I think you might have cracked a rib there . . . and

there,' she pressed. 'You might need some X-Rays.' She
glanced over at the girl. 'If you'll wait here, the doctor will
be along to you shortly.'

The girl nodded. 'Of course. Thank you very much.'

With a final glance into the young woman's face, Aisling
Miller ducked out of the cubicle, pulling the curtain over
behind her. There was something about that couple—and
about the girl in particular—that rang a vague bell in her
memory.

Judith looked at Spider and pressed her fingers to her lips.
She parted the cubicle curtain slightly and watched the
young nurse talking to a white-coated doctor. They both
looked towards the cubicle and Judith ducked back

They had made two stupid mistakes, she knew that now.
She shouldn't have claimed that they were brother and
sister . . . their accents alone gave that away. And they
shouldn't have claimed that Spider had fallen off a
motorbike; his wounds weren't consistent with that. Anyway
there was nothing they could do for the moment except
brazen it out. The nurse might be curious, but that didn't
mean that she was going to do anything.

The cubicle curtain swept back and the doctor—dark-
haired, dark-eyed, looking no older than Spider—bustled in.
Judith noticed the way he immediately looked at her rather
than at the patient, and she knew then that they were in
trouble. The young nurse came in moments later and stood
by the doctor's side. She too was watching Judith closely.

'So, young man, you came off a motorbike. What speed
were you doing?'

'Thirty . . . forty . . . something like that,' Spider said
tightly. He could sense Judith's unease, and that alone made
him nervous. He was out of place here, but this was her
world, and he was quite willing to allow her to make the
decisions. However, his own instincts were telling him to run.

The doctor examined the wound on his forehead and

then peered into his eyes with a small torch. 'Any pain,' he muttered, 'nausea, double-vision, ringing in your ears?'

'Nothing. I've a headache,' he added.

'I'm not surprised,' the doctor grinned. 'That's some bang you got yourself.' He glanced back over his shoulder at Judith. 'We'll have it X-Rayed just in case, but I don't think there's anything wrong.'

Judith nodded.

The doctor then pressed Spider's ribs, tracing them with the tips of his fingers. At one point Spider hissed with pain.

'I don't think it's broken, probably cracked. But we'll have that X-Rayed too, nurse.'

'Yes, doctor.'

'We'd like you to stay in overnight just to keep an eye on that head wound,' he added, looking from Spider to Judith.

They both looked at one another, and Judith said, 'Is that absolutely necessary?'

'It is recommended. Is there a problem?' he asked smoothly.

'No problem,' Judith countered. 'Of course Simon will stay.' She was looking at Spider as she spoke, her eyes wide, willing him to say nothing. Spider started to shake his head, but Judith's fixed glare silenced him.

Aware that something was going on between the two, the doctor simply smiled and glanced back over his shoulder at the nurse. 'Perhaps if we got those X-Rays sorted out . . . ?'

'Of course, doctor.'

The young doctor slapped Spider on the shoulder. 'You're a very lucky young man. I'll look in on you later on.'

Spider started to thank him, but he brushed through the curtains, followed a moment later by the nurse.

As soon as they had left, Spider slid off the plastic covered bench and reached for his t-shirt. 'I'm getting out of here.'

'Hang on a sec,' she muttered. She was peering through the curtain, watching the doctor and nurse talking together. The doctor nodded, and the nurse moved towards the reception desk. She spoke to the young woman behind the desk, who immediately lifted up the phone. Both the receptionist and the nurse were looking towards the cubicle. 'We're getting out of here now,' she said quickly. 'Whose idea was it to come here in the first place?'

'Yours, if I remember correctly,' Spider said with a quick smile.

'It wasn't the best idea I ever had,' Judith admitted.

'I know.' Spider pulled on his leather jacket. With his left arm cradling his sore ribs, and his right hand on Judith's shoulder, they slipped out from behind the curtain and were making their way towards the swinging doors when they heard a shout behind them. They ignored it and kept walking.

'Stop . . . you two, stop!'

The young nurse ran up and stood in front of them. 'Just where do you think you're going?' she demanded.

'Out of my way,' Spider snapped.

But the nurse was looking at Judith and suddenly her eyes widened in recognition. 'I know you . . .' she hissed. 'I know you.'

Spider brushed past the woman and manoeuvred Judith down the hall. The nurse made a grab for his arm, but Spider snarled at her, baring his teeth like a wild animal, and she backed away. 'Help . . . Help . . .' She was pointing at the couple. 'Stop them. She's Judith Meredith . . .'

Footsteps pattered close-by, and Judith leaned closer to Spider. 'Can you run?'

'No, not really.'

'We don't have a choice.'

Gritting his teeth, holding tightly onto Judith, Spider ran. Behind them they could hear the nurse screaming.

Tuesday 31st July

13

MASSIVE POLICE HUNT
FOR KIDNAPPED HEIRESS

A massive police hunt was on today for the kidnapped heiress, Judith Meredith, the daughter of industrialist Maxwell Meredith. The search is concentrated in the Midlands area, where the fifteen-year-old girl was spotted by a sharp-eyed nurse in Mullingar Hospital.

Nurse Aisling Miller said, 'I spotted them the moment they came into Casualty. The young man was cut about the face and had obviously been in a fight. The girl was pale faced and obviously terrified. He was very nervous and, following the examination by the doctor when he learned that he would have to stay in overnight, he grabbed the young girl and dragged her from the hospital.'

Police are looking for a pale blue Hiace van, with two or possibly more people travelling in it. The young man is said to be bruised about the face and may be wearing a bandage around his forehead. Anyone with information is asked to contact . . .

Maxwell Meredith flung down *The Irish Times* and glared at the police inspector. 'I thought we agreed no newspapers, no reporters.'

The inspector shrugged. 'Someone in the hospital talked. It's difficult—if not impossible—to keep something like this under wraps. And, in a roundabout way, this might actually work to our advantage. Someone might see the van; they'll certainly be on the look-out for them now—and the boy will be difficult enough to miss. I'm confident we'll have them soon.'

Frankie reached up and took her husband's hand, squeezing the fingers slightly, attempting to calm him down. She was sitting in the fireside chair directly across from the inspector and when she smiled at the senior Garda, he actually blushed, the tips of his ears turning a bright red. 'Inspector, in my experience, the newspapers only tell half the story, and the police only tell you what they want you to know anyway. Would you care to fill us in on the details?'

'Well, ma'am, that's true: there is a little more to this case than meets the eye.' He indicated the newspapers lying scattered around the floor. 'I know the papers are calling this a kidnap, but I've spoken to both the nurse and the doctor who attended the injured boy, and they were both quite insistent that Judith was under no constraint; in fact they both seemed to think that she had been in charge.'

'Impossible,' Maxwell snapped.

Ignoring him, the inspector pressed on. 'Both witnesses describe the boy as having an itinerant accent . . . indeed that's what gave the pair away originally. She—that is your daughter—claimed that they were brother and sister when, of course, their accents told an entirely different story. Both witnesses agree that the girl was making the decisions; the boy—he gave his name as Simon, but we have reason to believe that this was a false name—kept looking to her for instructions and directions. She did the talking for them both.' He looked directly at Maxwell Meredith, his face impassive. 'I am inclined to believe that your daughter was not kidnapped, sir. The evidence suggests that she has run away!'

'Impossible! How would she meet this . . . this itinerant in the first place, eh?'

The inspector stood and picked up his hat. 'When we catch her, we'll ask her.'

14

Spider came slowly and painfully awake. His head was a solid ball of agony and he had difficulty focusing properly. Every breath he took sent slivers of pain deep into his lungs. He'd been hurt before, in fights, in accidents, he'd survived bitter winters and he'd known the gut-wrenching pangs of hunger, but he'd never experienced anything like this. He attempted to sit up, but the pain whipped through his body and he moaned involuntarily.

Judith was by his side immediately. She wrapped her arms around him, drawing him close to her. Her dirty face was smudged and streaked, and her eyes were red-rimmed. 'Spider,' she whispered hoarsely, 'I'm sorry, I'm so, so sorry. I got you into this. This is all my fault.'

Spider had to wet his lips with his tongue before he could speak. His voice was a rasp. 'Stop that. This had nothing to do with you.' He attempted to smile, but his cracked, dry lips refused to obey.

'This is your bad luck theory?' She brushed tears from her cheeks with the back of her hand.

'If it's going to get you . . .' he croaked. He eased himself upright in the seat. 'Where are we?'

Judith shook her head. 'I don't know. We passed through a place called Kilcatherina before I stopped for the night.'

'What happened when we left the hospital?' Spider asked, 'I really don't remember . . .'

'We made it to the van and you drove away at high speed. We drove about a mile, but your forehead started bleeding again and we were weaving all over the road. I changed places with you—you were practically asleep at the wheel. I took the first side road I could find and then kept to the minor roads driving on through the night. I got lost a couple of times, and sometimes the roads were so narrow I thought I'd get stuck. Finally I got so tired I had to stop.'

Spider nodded . . . and immediately wished he hadn't. His head throbbed. 'What did you say the name of that village was?' he asked.

'Kilcatherina.'

'I know it. The next major town is Moate, and then onto Athlone, Ballinasloe, Loughrea and Galway . . . if we stick to the main roads. We could cut across country though . . .'

Judith gripped his face in her small hands and turned it so that she was looking directly into his black eyes. 'You're going nowhere. You need medical attention.'

'I need rest.'

'We'll go back to Dublin. I'll explain everything to my father. He'll get you the best treatment.'

Spider's laugh subsided into a groan. 'You're only fooling yourself, Judith. He'll be delighted to see you. But not so pleased to see me. No . . . let me get some rest and I'll be fine then.'

'You're hurt,' Judith hissed, feeling tears of rage sparkle in her eyes. 'You're hurt because of me, and I want to see you well again. We should have stayed in that hospital. I don't know why we ran away. We've done nothing wrong.'

'The police would have been called,' Spider stated flatly. 'I don't want to get involved with the police.'

'But Spider, you're innocent. Your crime was helping me!'

Spider sighed. 'The police have little love for the travellers, especially the young crowd like me. And what's it going to look like to them, eh? A young girl from a rich family with an itinerant boy who hasn't got a couple of pence to rub together. What'll they think? What can they think?'

Judith released Spider and picked up the newspaper she had bought, along with some food and cans of coke in a tiny shop in Kilcatherina, late the previous night. She handed him *The Irish Times*, folded open to the story about the kidnapping.

Spider took it from her, squinting at the blurring letters, and then he pointed to the photograph. 'That's you.'

'That's me,' she agreed. She rummaged through the plastic bag at her feet, pulled out a carton of pure orange juice and shook it vigorously. 'I think you had better read the story though.'

Spider looked at the paper for a few moments before handing it back to her. 'You read it to me.'

'Your eyes!' Judith whispered. 'Can you see? Are you seeing double?'

'I can't read,' he said very quietly. 'I told you that,' he added, almost accusingly.

Judith looked at him blankly. 'You told me you couldn't write,' she said very slowly, 'I thought you were talking about your handwriting.'

'I can neither read nor write,' he mumbled, not looking at her. 'Oh, I can recognise simple things, words, sentences, brand names, town and village names, but I can't read.'

'But everyone can read.'

The young man reached over and took her hand, the spider tattoo on the back of his hand seeming to curl around her fingers. 'No, Judith, not everyone. When you're living by the side of the road, when you're moving from place to place, when all your energies are concentrated on simply surviving, then things like schooling, like reading and writing just don't seem so important.'

'How old are you, Spider?' Judith asked.

He looked at her, his gaze steady and then he said slowly, 'Seventeen.'

'Seventeen,' she repeated. Judith Meredith couldn't conceive of a life without being able to read. Why, she couldn't even remember a time when she hadn't been able to read. 'But I thought your parents were settled,' she said, puzzled.

Spider squeezed her fingers. 'I just never got around to it. There never seemed to be enough time. I hated school. I didn't want to learn . . . after a while I suppose the teachers stopped trying to teach me.'

'But Spider . . . you'll have to learn how to read. How are you going to get a job if you can't read?'

Spider started to laugh. He stopped abruptly when both his head and ribs protested. 'Judith, do you know what the unemployment rate is amongst the travelling community? Even if I could read and write, the very fact that I'm a traveller with no fixed address ensures that many—no, most—jobs are closed to me.'

'But how will you survive?' She was appalled by the prospect presented to her of the young man, seventeen years old, with no future in store for him. Her own career had been planned out years ago.

'There's always seasonal work around harvest time, picking potatoes and fruit, that type of thing, though more and more students are getting into that line. I can earn a bit of money dealing in car parts, trading horses, doing odd jobs. And of course, there's the dole.' He suddenly reached up and touched her cheek with his forefinger, wiping away the tears. 'Why are you crying?'

'There has to be more,' she said fiercely.

Spider shook his head. 'There isn't.' He gathered the weeping girl into his arms, puzzled and confused by her emotional outburst. 'Why should it upset you?'

'Because I care about you. Because I love you!'

In the long silence that followed, Spider slowly released her hand. He pushed her away from him gently, holding her at arm's length. He started to shake his head, ignoring the pounding in his skull. 'You can't do that,' he whispered, appalled.

'Do what?'

'Love me.' He shook his head savagely, ignoring the pain. 'You can't love me.'

'Why not?'

Spider looked at her, at a loss for an answer. 'Because . . . because you've only known me for three days.'

'How long do you have to know someone before you decide that you love them?' she smiled. 'I know you don't love me, I don't expect that, but I just wanted you to know that I love you enough to care for you.' She sat back, blinking furiously, determined not to allow the tears to flow again. Folding her arms across her chest, she could feel the pounding of her heart beneath her right hand.

In the long silence that followed, Spider said simply, 'I do.'

'What?' she asked, turning to look at him. He was huddled in the corner, slumped against the passenger door, looking smaller than she remembered him. 'What did you say?'

'I do love you,' he said slowly, very quietly. 'But I didn't even want to think about it, because I never thought that someone like you could ever care for someone like me.'

'Oh Spider,' she sighed. She slid across the seat and wrapped her arms around him, drawing him close. He felt cold, and she could feel him shivering through the thin t-shirt. She looked down into his face, into his deep-set black eyes and she felt something swell up inside her that caught at her breath, sent her heart tripping madly, sent tingles running through her fingers. She even had difficulty breathing. 'There is no-one like you, Spider,' she whispered, running her fingers down the soft stubble on his cheeks.

'I've never met anyone like you,' he said softly, finally putting into words what he'd been thinking. 'You're a remarkable woman, Judith Meredith.'

A warm glow spread upwards towards her cheeks. No-one had ever called her a woman before. She ran the back of her hand across his bruised cheek and then traced the line of his lips with her forefinger. 'I'm not remarkable, Spider, don't be silly.'

He nipped at her finger with his strong white teeth. 'Oh, but you are. Think of what you've done in the past few days . . . running away, rescuing me, taking charge now that I'm hurt. I think there's very few women of your age who would be able to do that. You are remarkable, Judith.'

'If I'm remarkable, then you've made me that way. You've allowed me to see a side of myself that I never knew existed. I didn't know what life was all about until I met you, Spider . . .' She leaned forward and kissed him lightly on the lips. 'You've made me feel like a woman.'

15

The Garda inspector arrived at the Merediths' Killiney house just as the Nine O'Clock News was beginning on RTE 1. He brushed past the housekeeper as he heard the newsreader's calm measured tones begin to list the day's calamities and disasters. As the tall, grey-haired man hurried into the room, he realised he was too late . . .

Seated before the large colour television set, Maxwell and Frankie watched in horrified silence as the female newsreader read out the latest developments in the Judith Meredith kidnapping.

The camera cut to a shot of a young wild-haired woman standing in the middle of a caravan site. Although she was talking to a young reporter, she kept glancing nervously at the camera.

'. . . he was always wild, always in trouble with the law. There's hundreds of witnesses,' she continued. 'He must have picked her up in Dublin, and brought her here. She was terrified of him, you could see that. We all knew there was something wrong . . . sure what would a lady like that want with someone like him? He ran out yesterday morning, taking her with him. I think he knew things were getting too hot for him.'

'And what happened then, Miss Ryan?'

'My brothers and myself were heading into Kinnegad later in the morning . . .'

'Monday morning?'

'Aye, yesterday morning. We were driving along when we saw Spider's van parked by the side of the road. We stopped in case anything had happened to it. We got out to help. But Spider attacked us. He was like a wild animal. He stole our van and drove off in the direction of Kinnegad.'

'We've heard reports that Spider may have been injured in a fight; would you know anything about that?'

'Aye. He threatened me with a knife, but my brothers came to my rescue. There was a bit of a punch-up, but that Spider . . . he's vicious.'

'Have you any idea where they are now, Miss Ryan?'

The young woman shook her head. 'No. I feel sorry for the girl though. God knows what she's going through.'

Maxwell Meredith snapped off the television and turned to face the inspector. He was white-faced and shivering, his lips drawn into a thin bloodless line. 'I would have preferred to have heard this from you, Inspector Doyle,' he snapped.

'I was coming here to tell you myself. I only learned on the way over that it had been leaked to the press.'

'I thought we agreed no publicity . . . especially publicity of this type.' He jerked his thumb at the television.

'We did. The young woman in the interview contacted the local papers and RTE and "sold" them exclusive interviews.'

Maxwell turned to look at his wife, and it was Frankie who asked the question he couldn't. 'Is what she says true, inspector?'

The big man sat down in a chair facing the couple. 'Yes . . . and no,' he said eventually. He held up his hand as Maxwell and Frankie both opened their mouths to ask questions. 'We've made extensive enquiries, and it turns out that Judith arrived at the camp in the company of a young man called Sean, nicknamed Spider, O'Brien, on Sunday morning. They were having trouble with their van and it had

106

to be towed into the camp. They left early Monday morning, and we found the O'Brien lad's van outside Kinnegad as the young lady said. We made some enquiries in the town and a young woman, fitting the description of your daughter, was seen buying groceries there. So far, everything fits. The next sighting we have is when they turn up in the hospital.'

'But what about this lout who's kidnapped her?' Maxwell demanded.

'We have no evidence that she has actually been kidnapped. All the evidence to hand seems to suggest that she went with him of her own accord. Apparently she remained alone in the van on Sunday while he went to the camp to arrange to be towed in. She slept in one of the women's caravans that night. We think that she went into Kinnegad while Spider attempted to repair the van. If he had kidnapped her, then she wouldn't have this amount of freedom.'

'But what about the young woman . . . ?'

'People say and do things in order to appear on television,' he smiled. 'And you don't want to believe every-thing you hear on the news. Anyway, we interviewed the girl and her two brothers at length and, in my estimation, her story is a fabrication. We have evidence that Spider had been involved in a fight; according to the girl, he fought with her two brothers, but there isn't a mark on either lad. I think they attacked Spider; maybe they wanted to return your daughter for the reward.'

'And the young man, this Spider O'Brien?' Frankie asked quietly. 'Do you know anything about him?'

'We know him. Seventeen years old. Been on the streets since he was ten. He's from a travelling background, but his parents settled shortly after he was born. He's been done for vagrancy, petty theft—usually food or sweets—driving with no insurance, no licence, no tax, that sort of thing. He's got a bit of a reputation on the streets as a fighter, but he's very much a loner. If it's any consolation, he doesn't do drugs as far as we know, although he drinks occasionally, and he's not involved in crime.' He looked from Frankie to Maxwell. 'I don't think he's kidnapped your daughter.'

'Have you any idea where they are now?'

The inspector shook his head. 'They seem to be heading into the west. The Galway races are on at the moment; we're speculating that Spider may have some relatives over for the races. A lot of travelling families use it as a way of keeping in contact. Have you any relations in Galway that Judith might run to?'

Maxwell started to shake his head and then stopped. He looked at his wife with wide eyes.

'Jean,' they both said simultaneously.

The inspector pulled out his notebook and looked at them expectantly.

'Jean Ashe,' Maxwell explained, 'my late wife's sister, Judith's aunt. She has a house in Salthill, overlooking Galway Bay. She . . . she didn't really get on with Frankie and she didn't attend the wedding . . .' He paused. It was now Tuesday night; had they only married on Saturday? It seemed like a lifetime ago. He scribbled the address and telephone number on the back of a business card. 'She might go there,' he said, feeling his own excitement beginning to build up inside him. 'She always got on well with her aunt.'

'Don't pin too many hopes on it, sir. It's just a possibility.'

'That's more than we've had so far,' Maxwell Meredith said feelingly.

The inspector stood up and slid his notebook into his pocket. 'We will keep you in touch with developments.'

Maxwell saw the inspector to the door, and waited until he had driven away. When he returned to the sitting-room, he looked more relaxed, and some of the tension had gone from his shoulders.

'At least we know where she's going,' Frankie said brightly.

Maxwell nodded. 'That's some consolation. I'd be happier knowing where she is right now though,' he whispered.

16

Even though it was the first of August, the early morning air was bitterly cold. Spider and Judith huddled together in the back of the van, an old blanket tucked in around their shoulders beneath their chins, newspapers wrapped around their feet. They had run the engine every half hour to heat up the van, but had stopped when their fuel ran low, and they didn't know how far they were from the nearest petrol station.

Spider had dozed on and off throughout the day. His sleep had been troubled and Judith was afraid that he was running a fever. The gash on his forehead had turned an ugly purple and had swelled up into a egg-shaped lump. His face was a mass of purple-green bruises. He had moaned in his sleep, tossing and turning, sometimes so violently that he had actually awoken with the pain in his ribs. They had made their plans the last time he had come fully awake. They would fill up the van with fuel at the first petrol station they came to and drive straight into Galway. Spider was now feeling so ill that he had actually agreed to allow Judith to get him a doctor there. They both knew that this would probably be their last night together.

'Are you awake?'

Judith stirred and squinted into the darkness. Spider was a barely recognisable shape beside her. 'I'm awake. I thought you were asleep,' she muttered. She could feel the heat radiating from his body, and the solid, rapid thrumming of his heart beneath her fingers. 'You should try and sleep,' he said quietly. 'You need the rest.'

'I've rested all day. How do you feel?' she asked.

He shifted slightly, easing a cramped arm. 'Bruised, battered, sore. But I feel much better.'

'How's your head?'

'Feels like I've been up all night drinking.'

'You don't drink, do you?' she asked, surprised.

Spider laughed gently . . . and immediately wished he hadn't: the sound echoed inside his head. 'You know, just when I think I'm getting to know you, you say or do something that makes me realise I'll probably never know you.'

She shook her head slightly. 'I don't know what you mean.'

Spider's hand closed over hers and he squeezed the fingers gently, pressing it to his chest. 'I'll bet you've never been drunk in your life.'

'Of course not!' she said, horrified at the very thought.

'Have you ever drunk alcohol?'

'I've had a glass of wine with my meals . . .' she said slowly. 'I've drunk shandy too a couple of times. I didn't really like it though,' she added.

'Why did you drink it then?'

Judith shrugged. 'My friends were trying it.'

Spider began to laugh softly.

'What's so funny?' she asked.

'Nothing's funny. Nothing at all. When I was living on the streets, I met lots of people who started to drink because their friends were drinking, or who started taking drugs because their friends were using and they didn't want to be left out. Some of the "friends" I made on the streets wanted me to drink or use, but I decided they weren't real friends.'

'But you drink,' Judith said, confused.

'Lots of travellers drink, Judith,' he said very quietly. 'Because you can escape in a bottle. All the problems that surround you, that are a part of your life when you're a traveller, cease to exist. The bottle makes you feel as if you're someone.'

'You don't need a bottle to be someone,' she said very softly, realising that he was talking about himself.

'What future is there for me and the people like me,' he asked bitterly.

'Spider, you're tired. Don't even think about it.'

'Just because you're able to take care of yourself, just because you don't back down from a fight, people think you don't need anyone. But you get lonely sometimes.' She saw his face, an indistinct shape in the night, turn to face her. 'The drink takes the pain away, takes the loneliness away.'

Judith felt her throat beginning to burn, and she was suddenly glad that it was dark in the van and that he couldn't see the tears on her face.

'I've only known you for three days, Judith, but I don't think I've ever spent that length of time in the one place or with the one person since I left home. Travelling comes to be a habit,' he continued, the pale blur of his face turning away from her. 'You keep moving on . . . looking for something.'

'What are you looking for, Spider?' she asked, her voice barely above a whisper. Beneath her hand she could feel his heart begin to pound faster.

'I broke my mother's heart when I ran away from home.' He wasn't talking to her now, Judith knew. It was as if he were thinking aloud. 'But I always came back home; I always had a home to come back to. And then my mother died.' There was a long pause, which Judith was almost afraid to break. 'My father once told me I had sent my mother into an early grave . . . maybe he was right. I walked away the day of her funeral; I've never been back. There was nothing to go back to. I love travelling, always have. It's in my blood you see, but I always loved coming home . . . having someone to come home to. I could always go home to my mother. It was my safety net. When things got too bad, when I couldn't stand the streets any more, she was always there. Waiting. She loved me, you see. No matter what I did, she still loved me.' There was another long pause, and then Spider added softly, 'That's what you miss on the road, when you're travelling alone . . . love.'

Judith tightened her hold on him. 'But you've got me now. I love you, Spider,' she said fiercely.

Spider shook his head quickly. 'No . . . no you cannot, Judith. Maybe you like me . . . maybe you're grateful to me. But I've thought about it: you cannot love me.'

'Why not?' she asked, horrified.

'Because there's no future for us. You have a future, Judith; you can read and write, you know what you're going to be. You'll have a career, a house of your own, a husband and children if you want them. I don't have a future. I can neither read nor write, I'll probably never have a place of my own that doesn't have wheels . . .' his voice trailed away.

'And what about a wife and children, Spider?' Judith asked.

'Probably.'

'Probably? You sound almost resigned to it.'

'I've told you, Judith, travelling can be a desperately lonely occupation. After a while you need someone to share it with.'

'Could you not share with me?'

Spider nodded. 'I could . . . if things were different.'

'What things? What is keeping us apart?' she demanded.

'Too much money, too many years of prejudice.' He squirmed around in the seat, and she felt his warm hands come up to cup her face. When he spoke his breath was warm on her lips. 'Listen to me, Judith Meredith,' he said earnestly. 'I've learned a lot from you in the last few days. You've made me look at things differently; I'd like to think that you've learned a little from me too. Maybe you'll look a little more sympathetically on the next traveller you see begging on the street, or maybe you won't turn up your nose as you drive past an encampment. I love you, Judith Meredith, but you cannot love me. We cannot love one another.' His lips, cool and dry, like paper, brushed across her cheek. 'Tomorrow we'll be in Galway, and then I'll never see you again.'

'Spider,' Judith whispered, pressing her lips to his, kissing him fiercely. She hugged him close, only releasing him when she heard him grunt with pain. 'Spider, I'll never forget you.' She kissed him again, tasting moisture on his cheeks.

'And I'll never forget you, Judith Meredith,' he promised.

Wednesday 1st August

17

They had intended setting out at first light, but neither awoke until just after nine. They had slept in each other's arms, warm and comfortable in one another's presence. Judith had fallen asleep with her head on Spider's chest, listening to the steady, reassuring throb of his heart, while his long fingers had gently stroked her hair.

Judith's last conscious thought before sleep finally claimed her was the realisation that love changed your perspective. When she'd left home, she'd been thinking only of herself . . . she hadn't even taken the time to consider how her father felt, how he must be feeling. But she hadn't known then what it was like to be in love. She wondered if her feelings for Spider were anything like her father's feelings for Frankie. If they were, then how could she blame her father for marrying the woman?

Love changed everything . . .

'Time to go.'

Judith came awake with a start. Spider was bending over her, his big dark eyes inches away from hers. He kissed her gently on the forehead, but she raised her face to meet his lips with hers. 'Time to go,' he murmured.

'Do you feel any better?' she asked.

'I've felt worse.'

'Will you still let me get you a doctor when we reach Galway?'

He playfully squeezed the end of her nose between thumb and forefinger. 'I promised, didn't I?'

Judith straightened, rubbing the heels of her palms into her eyes, blinking out into the misty morning. They had parked close into the hedge in a narrow country lane. Trees lined both sides of the road, meeting in an arch overhead. Down the centre of this leafy tunnel, grey-white fog twisted and curled. Judith cracked open the door on her side and stepped down into the chill morning, shivering slightly, swinging her arms from side to side, stamping her feet. Her breath plumed whitely on the air before her. Spider hopped down behind her and drew her into his arms, hugging her close. She wrapped her arms around him, feeling the heat from his body soak into hers. Finally, he released her and held her at arm's length. 'Let me look at you.'

'You can look at me all day,' she grinned.

Spider shook his head. 'I mightn't get another chance. Things could get a bit hairy today. Kathleen's nasty enough to have gone to the police and reported the van stolen. We already know the police are looking for you, and they'll have got a description from the hospital. They also know we're headed in this general direction.'

'Are you saying they could be waiting for us?'

He shrugged. 'Maybe.'

'What do we do then?'

'What do you want to do?'

'I want to be with you.'

Spider laughed. 'I meant what do you want to do if we come up to a police checkpoint.'

'Do we have a choice?' she asked, surprised.

'Of course we've a choice. It all depends on how much warning we have. It's easy to spot a checkpoint in the city because there's usually a string of cars stopped in front of it, but in the country you can be on them before you know it. If we see it in time, we can turn around, or turn off the road, or we can brazen it out. What do you want to do?'

Judith shook her head. 'I don't know. I've never done this sort of thing before.'

Spider drew her into his arms again. 'To be honest, neither have I.'

'What do you want to do?' she asked.

'I want to deliver you to your aunt's house in Galway. That's what we started out to do . . . let's try to finish that.'

Judith stood on her toes to kiss him. 'Let's do that then.'

They passed through Kilcatherina just after ten, but decided not to stop. She had been in the town once before to buy food and drink, but that had been late at night when people were tired and less likely to remember her. But she would certainly be remembered if she went through there a second time. They made the same decision when they came to Kilnahinch, and continued on the few miles into Moate. Moate was on the main road into Athlone and en route for Galway and they imagined they would escape unnoticed there. They used the last of Judith's money and bought themselves a breakfast of sorts—cartons of fresh orange juice, a French loaf, some cooked ham and tomatoes, and a small tub of margarine. Judith also bought *The Irish Times* and the *Independent*, both of which were carrying front page stories about the Judith Meredith kidnapping. The two papers carried the same picture of her, but there was absolutely no resemblance between the magnificently dressed, beautifully made-up girl in the photograph and the rather dirty, dishevelled young woman she'd become.

They stopped on the long flat road outside Moate and Judith read the newspaper reports while Spider made enormous sandwiches.

'You were right about Kathleen,' she said quietly. She turned the paper so that Spider could see a photograph of Kathleen flanked by her two brothers.

He looked at the photograph for a few moments and she saw his expression change, harden, his eyes turn cold and distant. She wondered what would happen if he ever caught up with them . . . and then decided that she didn't want to know.

'What does it say?'

'It says you have kidnapped me, that you attacked her with a knife when they attempted to rescue me, and that you beat up her brothers and then stole their van. She describes you as "an animal",' she finished quietly.

'I'd need to be Superman to have done all that,' he remarked.

Judith folded the paper in half to read the last few paragraphs. 'It says here that police have mounted an intensive search in the Midlands and are currently looking for a pale blue Hiace van, registration number . . .' her voice trailed away.

Spider shrugged. 'Do you know how many pale blue Hiaces there are in Ireland?'

'What about the registration?'

'I'll cover it with mud,' he said immediately.

'Do you have a solution for everything?' she asked.

'Most things,' Spider shrugged. 'I've told you before: there are things you have some control over, others you have no control over. I learned how to tell the difference between the two a long time ago. If you've no control over something, then why bother even worrying about it?'

'It's a marvellous philosophy.'

'Fil . . . fil . . .'

'Philosophy. A way of thinking, a way of seeing things.'

'Sounds like a fancy name for common sense.' He passed her across her sandwich and they ate in silence, drinking fresh orange juice straight from the cartons. It was delicious; she had never tasted food quite like it before. When they were finished, she wiped her fingers on her jeans. She stopped suddenly, realising how natural the action had been.

'What's so funny?' Spider asked.

'I was just thinking how easily I've forgotten my manners.'

'This is the real world,' he said around a mouthful of bread. 'You don't need manners to survive in the real world.'

Judith nodded solemnly. Was her world so false . . . or was it just that Spider's world was all too real? She looked up at Spider and smiled, realising that was why she liked him: he was a real person. There was no pretence about him, no false airs. She had seen the look that came into his eyes when she had told him about Kathleen. His anger, his disgust, had been real, undisguised. Someone from her world would be upset if they learned that a friend had just betrayed them. They'd talk about him, moan about it, but probably do nothing . . . maybe they'd never speak to them again. Spider would do something about it.

And if he said he loved her . . . then he meant it.

Spider reached over and squeezed her hand. 'You've gone all quiet.'

'Do you love me, Spider?' she asked suddenly, surprising him. 'Just answer yes or no.'

'I love you,' he said simply, and turned the key in the ignition. Gravel spit from beneath the wheels as they pulled out onto the road.

Judith slid over as far as her seat belt would allow and rested her hand on his thigh. She didn't need any other answer.

They had passed through Athlone when Spider spotted the police car in his rear-view mirror. Judith immediately knew that something was wrong by the sudden tension in his arms.

'Duck down—now!'

Unsnapping the seatbelt, she slid down to the floor, aware now that her heart was pounding. She also realised that she didn't want the adventure to end . . . not now, not just yet.

Spider glanced at the speedometer and took his foot off the accelerator, allowing the van to slow to forty miles an hour. He knew this part of the road reasonably well. There was a turn off to the right which led to Belrea or a couple of miles beyond that a turn to the left which led down to Oldtown. If the police tried to stop him, he'd try to make one of the turnings and hope to lose them on the minor roads.

'Here they come,' he muttered.

The police car came up fast and he had a brief glimpse of three uniformed officers inside before it sped past without any of them even glancing into the van. Spider watched it disappear in the direction of Ballinasloe before he allowed Judith to resume her seat. 'Probably nothing,' he dismissed them. 'They've got bigger fish to fry.'

'It's not as if we're criminals,' Judith murmured.

'In their eyes we are,' Spider reminded her. 'And . . . eh . . . ' he tapped the steering wheel with the palm of his hand. 'We have stolen this van.'

'Well yes . . . but . . .'

'But nothing!' he grinned.

'I see a helicopter,' Judith said suddenly, leaning forward, squinting into the sky. The helicopter was a dot against the lowering clouds which had been threatening rain all morning.

'Could be army . . . could be fatcats heading into Galway for the races.' He glanced sidelong at Judith. 'Does your Da ever go to the Galway Races?'

'He's gone a few times, though he hates racing. But he takes clients there.' She smiled suddenly. 'And he always flies in by helicopter. I suppose that makes him a fatcat too?' she asked.

'Absolutely!'

'How far to Galway now?' she asked, attempting to read a sign as they flashed past. Large solid droplets of water spattered against the windscreen.

'Less than forty miles. We'll be there in an hour . . . an hour and a half at most.'

18

'And you're sure it was them?' The police inspector looked at each man in turn.

The three Gardaí looked at one another and then they nodded. The two on the left hand side of the car had been closest to the van and had got a good look at the driver. They were both convinced that it was Spider O'Brien.

'The registration had been covered over with mud, but the colour and type of van matched,' the driver said.

Inspector Doyle was sitting behind a desk in Ballinasloe Garda Station, where he was co-ordinating the attempt to catch up with Judith Meredith and Spider O'Brien. He had gambled that they would take the most direct route to Galway. Doubling the number of mobile units on the road, he had stationed men at strategic points on the route, and ordered two helicopter units into the air. He wanted this situation sorted out today—the press were having a field day with the 'kidnapping' theory, and were now beginning to discuss police competence, and were questioning his own ability to handle the situation. No spoilt brat was going to spoil thirty years of solid police work. Today was her last day of freedom.

Inspector Doyle stood up and turned to the large scale map he had pinned to the wall behind him. The route from Athlone to Ballinasloe and on to Loughrea was dotted with tiny coloured pins, each blue pin indicating the position of a man on the ground, the white pins representing the cars.

'Let's try and take them with the minimum of fuss and absolutely no publicity. The van has been sighted passing through Cornafulla and Ballydangan . . . the next stop is Woodmount . . .'

Even as he was speaking the radio on the desk crackled to life. '*Unit 21 to base. Come in please.*'

'This is base. Report please.'

'*Suspect van sighted driving through Woodmount on the N6 towards your position. Two occupants, young male and female. Registration illegible. Message ends. Over and out.*'

The inspector rubbed his large hands together, the sound rough and rasping. A broad grin broke his ruddy face. 'We have them now.' He looked at the three men. 'We'll pull the units in behind them and set up a road-block on the road between Ballinasloe and Aughrim.' He glanced at his watch. 'I hope they're enjoying their last hour together.'

19

His old instinct for trouble warned him that something was wrong. He had been uncomfortable since that police car had passed them outside Athlone without so much as a second glance. That was wrong. At the very least they should have pulled the van over and checked the tax and insurance. After all, it did match the type and colour of the van they were looking for. And Spider knew that while the Gardaí might be many things, they were not stupid. There had been three men in that car, and yet none of them had even glanced at the van . . . it was almost as if they were deliberately avoiding looking at it.

It was raining heavily now and the old ragged windscreen wipers left oily smears as they scraped across the glass, making it difficult—and sometimes impossible—to see through. If there were police watching the road, they were well concealed, and he hoped they were getting well and truly soaked for their trouble. As they had come through Woodmount, he had thought he'd seen a man in a car by the side of the road using a walkie-talkie, but he might have been mistaken.

The next town was Ballinasloe, and he had a couple of routes he could take there . . .

'What happens to us, Spider?' Judith said suddenly, interrupting his train of thought.

He glanced sidelong at her. She was sitting slumped in her seat, her arms folded across her chest. She looked ragged and dishevelled, badly in need of a wash, nothing at all like the artificially made-up young woman he had met four days ago. He thought she looked even prettier now.

'I mean,' she continued when he didn't immediately reply, 'what happens to us?'

Spider shrugged. He hadn't really thought about it. 'I don't know,' he said finally. 'I'll take you to your aunt's . . . and then I'll probably go on to the races and try to meet my uncle. I don't think I'll need to see a doctor after all,' he added quickly. 'My head is fine and my ribs only hurt if I breathe very deeply.'

'Spider—you promised!'

'I wasn't feeling well when I promised. I'm fine now. We travellers are sturdy, strong. It takes more than a few knocks to keep us down.'

Judith was silent for a few moments, and then she asked, 'Will I ever see you again?'

'Not unless you're thinking about running away again.'

'I might.'

'Don't even think about it,' he grinned. 'I don't think I could survive another four days with you.'

Judith punched his leg playfully. 'Be serious for a moment. Will I ever see you again?'

The windscreen wipers scraped across the glass while Spider thought about his answer. 'When I leave you at your aunt's, you'll be back in your world, and I'll drive back into mine. I don't think we'll ever meet again, Judith Meredith.'

'You sound so cold about it,' she almost accused him.

'Not cold. Realistic. In your world, you have friends for years, you see the same people day in and day out, you go to school with them, you live beside them, they become part of your life. When you're living on the road, you rarely get the opportunity to make those sort of friendships. You're always moving. You might stay in a camp for the winter, but come the spring you'll be on the road again and those people you met in the camp will go their way. You might never see them again.'

'When you're travelling from camp to camp, children move from school to school. They become used to relying on themselves and their immediate family. They don't bother making friends, because they know that sooner or later—and probably sooner—those friendships will be broken.' The scraping of the windscreen wipers had become an irritating rasp and he flicked it off. Within seconds it became impossible to see through the windscreen and he flicked it back on again. The scrape punctuated the silence.

'I've broken all the rules with you, Judith. I've let you get closer to me than anyone else I know . . .'

'Why was that?' she wondered.

'Maybe you don't make many friends when you're travelling, but you learn to make judgements about people . . . you have to if you're going to survive.'

'And what did you decide about me the day we met?'

'I decided you were a spoilt brat and trouble with a capital T,' he said with a grin.

'And now?'

'Well . . . you're still trouble with a capital T.'

Judith laughed. 'Be serious. Why did you let me get close to the real Spider?'

'I don't know. It just happened. I didn't mean it to happen; I certainly didn't want it to happen.'

'That's called love, I think.'

He nodded.

'You said you loved me, Spider . . . you sounded as if you meant it.'

'I meant it.'

'But you'll still let me go. You'll still walk away.'

Spider nodded. 'I'll let you go because I love you. I'll walk away because I love you.'

'But that's crazy . . .'

'Maybe it is. But what would your life be like if your friends knew you had a knacker for a boyfriend, an itinerant, a traveller, a gurrier, a punk?'

'That wouldn't bother me.'

'Maybe not in the beginning, but later it would. They'd make you a laughing stock, have nothing to do with you, and soon you'd come to hate me. I don't want that.'

'Will you write to me . . . I'm sorry,' she said immediately. 'I didn't mean . . . You could phone me though.'

Spider squinted through the streaked windscreen. They were coming into Ballinasloe. The streets were practically deserted, the few people who were out and about scurrying from shop to shop in the heavy rain. He didn't speak again until they had passed through the town. He had counted three police cars, all of them parked at side roads and turnings. He had noticed five uniformed men standing at intersections. As the van had driven by, he had watched them speak into their walkie-talkies. There would be a roadblock outside the town, he decided. There was a turning at Garbally, that would bring him across country to Portumna, but if he'd any money, he'd bet that road was blocked.

'What's wrong?' Judith asked softly, realising that his attention was elsewhere.

'Police . . . lots of police,' he said quietly, glancing in the rear view mirror. As he had expected, a dark blue car had pulled out behind them. He could just about make out the shapes of two heads. 'End of the road, Judith,' he said sadly.

She put her hand on his thigh, squeezing tightly. 'Does it have to be?'

'You know it does.' He glanced up into the murky sky, unsurprised to see the helicopter circling overhead. 'I'm sorry I couldn't bring you to your aunt.'

'You did your best.' She looked at him suddenly. 'Why did you want to do it anyway? Why did you want to bring me to Galway?'

He shrugged. 'It was just something I wanted to do. After a while I wanted to do it for you. I think it's probably the only time in my life I badly wanted to do something for someone else. For someone I cared about.'

'You sound as if it's all over.'

'It is.'

'So you'll just stop at the road-block? I thought you told me there were alternatives.'

He looked at her quickly. 'There are . . . but they're dangerous. And all they'll buy is is another few minutes . . .'

'Buy us those few more minutes, Spider. I want to be with you for as long as possible.'

The young Garda positioned at the junction in Garbally waited until the blue Hiace had driven past before radioing ahead. He watched while two unmarked cars carrying detectives drove by, and wished desperately he was positioned at the road block a few miles down the road. He wanted to be in at the capture of the guy who had kidnapped the heiress, Judith Meredith.

There were four police cars, two on either side of the road, just outside the village of Aughrim. When Inspector Doyle received the report from the Garda stationed in Garbally, he ordered the cars into position. Two cars blocked the road, bonnet to bonnet, while the other two would move in behind to block the van if it tried to turn. There were two carloads of detectives following it as well, and the inspector wasn't anticipating any trouble. He didn't think Spider was carrying any weapons, but the detectives were armed—just in case.

'Sir . . ?'

Inspector Doyle looked up in time to see the van appear in the distance, a vague blur in the rain. He lifted a pair of binoculars, but it was impossible to make out anything yet. 'Tell the lead car to move in,' he ordered the sergeant by his side. Moments later the radio crackled a response.

Judith squirmed around in the seat, glancing out through the rain-speckled rear window. 'They're not wearing uniforms.'

'They've been sitting on our tail for the past few miles, keeping exactly the same distance. They're police all right.'

'There's a second car behind them.'

'I'll bet you it's the same make of car.'

Judith looked back through the window again. 'I think you're right.' She turned back to Spider. 'What now?'

He nodded ahead. 'A road-block.'

She rubbed her hand across the windscreen, staring out at the dreary landscape. There were two police cars blocking the road. As she watched, their lights began to revolve, bathing the slick road in electric blue light. There seemed to be dozens of police standing about.

'Your welcoming committee,' he remarked.

'What did I do wrong, Spider?'

'You ran away,' he said simply. 'People from your background, with your money, don't have the freedom travelling people have. Money makes you an important person and the police look after important people.' The bitterness in his voice made her turn to look at him. She was shocked to find that his face had changed. Over the past few days, the tension had seeped from it, the lines had gone from his forehead and from around his eyes and lips. Now the lines were back, ageing him, hardening him, making his bruises livid. His lips were a thin white line, his eyes cold and hard. This was the Spider she had first known. 'I think I should stop . . .' he suggested.

'Don't stop,' she said.

Spider eased his foot off the accelerator and switched on his hazard lights. The flicking orange lights coloured the rain-water, competing with the colder blue of the police lights.

'Don't stop,' she pleaded.

'Shut up,' he snapped, and Judith recoiled with the anger in his voice. She was losing him, she knew, he was moving back into his world, a cold, friendless, often dangerous world.

Spider watched the speedometer drop: thirty-five . . . thirty . . . twenty-five . . . twenty. He eased down through the gears until he was gliding along in second gear. He was about a hundred yards from the road-block, and already he could see the Gardaí relaxing. There was what looked like a senior Garda standing by the side of the road, a broad smile on his ruddy face. Glancing in the mirror he saw that the two cars had taken up positions on either side of him. They thought he was going to give up.

What was it he had told Judith: every so often you make a decision that will change your life? The moment he had offered to take the girl to Galway he had made such a decision. He just hadn't known it at the time. Spider knew he didn't have much in the way of personal possessions, he didn't need them, but he had his own code, a simple, sometimes brutal code. It had earned him his reputation on the streets as being hard but fair: Spider was a good friend, but a bad enemy. And his word was good. He had made the girl a promise . . .

Twenty yards from the road-block, Spider stood on the accelerator.

The wheels spun on the slick road before taking hold. The van slewed from side to side as it built up speed, the engine howling in second gear. The cars which had been flanking them were left behind as the van surged away.

'Hang on!' he shouted.

'Spider!' Judith screamed, suddenly realising what he was going to do.

The van was travelling at nearly sixty miles an hour in third gear when it hit the two police cars at the point where they met in the centre of the road. The front of the van disintegrated under the blow, the headlights, bumper and bonnet crumpling into mangled metal, but the two police cars spun away on the wet roadway, leaving an opening through which the van scraped. Spider stood hard on the accelerator while working the gears, sending the van rocketing down the narrow road. He glanced into his rear-view mirror and smiled triumphantly at the confusion he had left in his wake. The cars carrying the detectives, caught unawares by Spider's sudden manoeuvre, had attempted to catch up with him. Unfortunately, they had been travelling too fast on the wet road when they had hit the remains of the road-block. The two cars ploughed into the already battered police cars and spun around and around on the wet road, creating an impassable barrier of twisted and broken metal and glass.

'Spider,' Judith said again, her voice coming in great breathy gasps. 'Spider.' Judith pressed her hand to her chest where she could feel her heart pounding.

'That was the alternative to stopping,' he grinned. 'You said you wanted a few more minutes.'

'I wanted us both alive to enjoy them,' she laughed shakily. She swivelled around in the seat, looking at the chaos they had left in their wake. 'That will hold them.'

'Not for long,' Spider muttered.

20

There was mud caked into the front of Inspector Doyle's blue uniform and his shoes were encased in thick balls of mud up to his ankles where he had dived into a ditch when the van had hit the road-block.

The Gardaí were wandering around, dazed, attempting to clear the wreckage from the road. Two of the cars were complete write-offs, and only one of the unmarked cars was drivable. The two cars he had kept in reserve were undamaged, but had been trapped behind the wreckage and were unable to pursue the van. Shading his eyes with his hand, Inspector Doyle could just about make out the black speck in the sky, where the helicopter was keeping track of the van.

He was totalling up the offences in his head as he reached for the walkie-talkie. There was little he could do with the girl: she would probably claim that she had been kid- napped . . . or rather, she would when her father had finished talking to her, since he certainly wouldn't want it known that his daughter had run away with an itinerant. But the boy was going to jail. Three Gardaí had been injured in the pile-up, one of them seriously. He looked down the road in the direction the van had taken: they wouldn't get through the next road-block so easily . . .

Spider drove through Aughrim and took a right turning that led towards Kilconnell. Privately he had very little hope of avoiding the police, but it had become a game now, with Judith's aunt in Galway as the prize. If he got her there, he won; if the police stopped them, they'd won.

'There's a helicopter overhead,' Judith said quietly. 'It's keeping track of us.'

'It'll take them time to get their act together,' Spider said tersely. 'They'll probably pull men in from Galway . . . and that helicopter can't stay up there forever; it'll have to refuel sooner or later. We still have a chance.'

They drove in silence for a while, and then Judith asked, 'Why did you do that, back there? You could have stopped, things wouldn't have been so bad.'

'You didn't want me to stop,' he said simply. 'You wanted a few more minutes . . .'

'I know all that,' she snapped, 'but . . .'

'But what?'

Judith looked at him, and then she said softly, 'I don't want you to get into any more trouble on my account.'

'I wanted to. You may have wanted a few more minutes . . . but I wanted that time too,' he admitted.

'Thank you,' she whispered. She looked at the narrow ribbon of road and sighed. 'Spider, this has got completely out of control; let's stop at the next police station and give ourselves up.'

Spider shook his head decisively. 'You're the one who wanted a few more minutes together, and what happens when I buy us those minutes . . . ? You want to use them to drive to the nearest police station.'

'I didn't realise how much those few minutes would cost. Up to the time we hit the police cars we were just inside the law.'

'Well, we've paid for those few minutes now . . . let's enjoy them.'

Judith remained silent for a while and then she said, 'How about if you get out of the van and walk away . . . I'll drive it to the nearest town and stop there, and they'll think I was driving the van when it hit the road-block . . .' She stopped when she saw the expression on his face.

'Let me finish what I started out to do, eh?' he snapped.

'Why?'

'Because I want to do something for you.'

'You've already done something for me . . . too much perhaps. I just wish I could have done something for you in return.'

'Do you love me?' Spider asked seriously, the question surprising her.

'Yes,' she said truthfully.

'Why?'

'Because . . . because . . . I do. I love you because you're you.'

'Then you've already done something special for me. It's been a long time since someone has loved me for no reason other than that they like me.'

'Lots of people must like you, Spider,' she said, surprised.

His sudden laughter was cold, almost angry. 'People fear me, Judith. I frighten them. They think that by liking me, I'll be on their side. I don't want that kind of liking or love, I don't need it.'

'I'm not frightened of you, Spider. But you frighten me sometimes. I'm afraid for you. But that's because I care for you.'

Spider ran the back of his left hand down the side of her face, tracing the line of her cheekbone. She kissed the backs of his fingers, and then reached down to unsnap the seatbelt and move over to kiss him . . .

The police officers who had been stationed in Ballinasloe had taken the A Road to Kilconnell as soon as news of the debacle outside Aughrim had come in on the radio. The reports spoke of a crazed and dangerous youth driving a stolen van at high speed. Officers had been injured and extreme caution was advised. The three police cars had driven at high speed, but with sirens off, and had arrived in the village of Kilconnell barely moments before the blue van, which had taken the minor road across country.

Spider came around the bend, travelling at forty miles an hour in fourth gear, wheels squeaking slightly on the wet ground. When he spotted the road-block his first instinct was to brake but instead he stood on the accelerator and dropped a gear. The van leapt away. Two of the police cars were parked at an angle on either side of the road with the third car facing them further down the road. There were two plainclothes detectives standing alongside the cars, both carrying small machineguns.

Judith was leaning across the front seat, her arm around Spider's narrow shoulders, when she saw the road-block. She squealed with fright and struggled back into her seat, attempting to clip her seatbelt closed.

Spider saw one of the detectives lift the gun and reacted instinctively. Wrenching the wheel to one side, he drove straight for the man, the van sliding from side to side. The detective threw himself to one side, rolling off the wet road.

Dimly aware that he was roaring and that Judith was screaming, Spider almost didn't hear the metallic knocking along the side of the van, but he felt the steering wheel twist and shift in his hand. He registered the image of the second detective, gun levelled at his hip, shooting at the back of the van. A tyre exploded, almost throwing the van across the road. It caught the edge of the first police car and seemed to climb up over it, to hang suspended in mid-air for a single horrifying moment before plunging down on top of the second car. Spider snatched at Judith as the van fell. She hadn't managed to close the seatbelt and there was a star-shaped crack in the windscreen where she had smashed her head. A thin trickle of blood was snaking down her forehead. He wrapped bloodied fingers around her jacket and attempted to hold her against the seat as the van slid off the second police car. When it hit the ground, it fell on the passenger side and slid along the wet surface, the windscreen dissolving, metal fragments breaking off in a cacophony of sound, jagged shafts of metal ripping up through the floor between the couple.

When the van finally stopped moving, the silence was an almost physical thing.

'Judith . . . ?' Spider whispered. The pain in his chest was almost unbearable, and he was twisted at an awkward angle, hanging out of the seat, only the seatbelt holding him in place. 'Judith?' His voice was a ragged croak, and he could taste the copper tang of blood in his mouth.

Judith was caught in a heap, lying atop the passenger door of the van 'below' him. Her face was a bloody mask from the cut on her forehead, and he could see that her left arm was twisted at an awkward angle. She didn't seem to be breathing.

'Judith?' He reached for her, but she was too far away. For the first time since his mother had died, there were tears in his eyes, and he felt that same sense of panic, of helplessness.

'Judith?' He was sobbing now, not realising it, the world lost in a blur of pain, his tears dropping down onto her face.

'JUDITH,' he screamed.

Fingers tightened into his.

Every movement was agony. There was fire in her head, in her chest, throbbing in her arm. She had heard her name called, vaguely, dimly, as if from a great distance, but she had followed the sound, regaining consciousness suddenly, aware of moisture on her cheeks, salt on her lips. She opened her eyes to find Spider above her, crying, his face surprisingly innocent, like a child's. Catching the edge of the seat, she attempted to stand, to crawl up to him.

'Judith,' he whispered, blinking hard. There were black spots at the edge of his vision.

She touched his face with her fingers, and then pressed her lips to his, holding him tightly, feeling the pain threatening to slide her back into unconsciousness.

'I . . . I . . . I love you, Spider,' she said, slipping away, falling out of his grasp.

His fingers tightened convulsively on her hand. 'I love you, Judith Meredith.'

When the two still bodies were pulled from the wreckage of the van, Spider's fingers were still locked around Judith's hand, the spider tattoo curled protectively around her soft flesh.

Thursday 2nd August

21

'Spider . . . Spider . . . SPIDER!'
Judith Meredith came awake with a scream and reared up in the bed. The pain was a bright solid light inside her head and she immediately lapsed back into unconsciousness. The next time she awoke she lay still, taking stock of her surroundings. She could smell the distinctive hospital odour. She breathed deeply, feeling her breath catch in her lungs with a sharp nick. There was an ache in her head that wasn't quite a pain, and there was no feeling in her left arm. When she lifted her right hand she could feel something pressing into it.

She opened her eyes . . . and found Frankie sitting beside the bed. The woman's hands closed over the girl's fingers. 'How do you feel?' she asked gently.

Judith managed a smile. 'How do I look?'

'Awful,' she smiled.

Judith licked dry lips. 'That's how I feel.'

'You're alive, sweetheart, that's all that matters.' Frankie stood up. 'I'll go and find your father . . .'

Judith caught Frankie's hand, squeezing it gently. 'Wait . . . wait a moment. I'm sorry Frankie. I didn't know . . .'

Frankie knelt on the floor and brought her head close to her step-daughter's. 'What didn't you know, Judith?'

Judith attempted a laugh, but it hurt her sides. 'I don't think I knew anything. I didn't know what it was like to love someone.'

'And now you do?'

'I do.'

Frankie leaned forward and kissed Judith on the cheek. 'Do you want to tell me about it . . . ?'

'There's not a lot to tell. After I . . . ran away, I met a boy . . . .' her voice trailed off into a whisper.

'We can talk about it when you're better,' Frankie murmured.

'I met a boy,' Judith continued as if she hadn't heard her. 'He was so different from anyone else I've ever met. He was kind and considerate . . . and he respected me as a person. He listened to what I had to say, allowed me to make my own decisions.'

'He sounds like a good boy,' Frankie said very quietly, realising that Judith wasn't listening to her.

'He showed me a way of life I never knew existed.' Judith's fingers tightened around her step-mother's. 'Do you know, he's seventeen years old, and he can barely read?' She paused, considering. 'But he had seen so much of life; he had done so many things . . . and yet, because of who he is and what he is, there's no future for him and the others like him.'

'He was an itinerant?'

Judith nodded. 'I just wonder what he'd be able to do if he had the opportunities that I have . . . '

'I think you fell in love with this young man,' Frankie said very quietly.

Judith nodded, tears sparkling in her eyes. 'I did.' She smiled up at her step-mother. 'Love makes you look at things in a different light. Makes you see things more clearly.'

'And what can you see clearly now?'

'I can see that you love Dad . . . and that he loves you.'

Frankie nodded. 'We do, Judith. We love one another very much.'

Judith's large brown eyes widened suddenly. 'Spider? What about . . . ?'

'Gone,' the older woman whispered. 'Disappeared during the night. He got up and walked away. The police are looking for him and I hope they don't catch him.'

'They won't,' Judith said proudly. 'He's a traveller.'

It came amongst the host of get well cards. The envelope was worn-looking, its edges stained and crumpled. Her name had been carefully spelt out in a thick heavy pencil, the letters crude and out of alignment. One of her nephews or nieces, she guessed.

There was a single page inside, torn from a copy book. Three words had been carefully etched onto the page . . . and they meant more to her than the hundreds of cards and presents she had received: